ecopunks

ecopunks

TONY BAILIE

For Anna Maris
best wishes
Tony Bailie

LAGAN PRESS
BELFAST
2010

This novel has been printed using paper approved
by the Forest Stewardship Council

Published by
Lagan Press
Unit 45
Westlink Enterprise Centre
30-50 Distillery Street
Belfast BT12 5BJ
e-mail: lagan-press@e-books. org. uk
web: lagan-press. org. uk

ISBN: 978 1 904652 91 5 (pbk)
978 1 904652 92 2 (hbk)
Author: Bailie, Tony
Title: ecopunks
2010

Set in Caslon

for Sinead

PART ONE

1

THE SOUND OF A COUGHING CHAINSAW spluttered to
life from within the forest. Another one started and then half a
dozen others followed by a chorus of grinding snarls as they came
into contact with tree trunks. Wolf, the tall bald man Madja had
been talking to, shushed her into silence. All around them the
sound of voices and laughter trailed off to be replaced by the
screech of metal on wood and the creak of emasculated trunks
teetering before crashing through the branches of other trees
around them and on to the ground. Madja started to push towards
the line of private security guards who had surrounded the ancient
oak forest and although Wolf tried to hold her back she pulled
away. Others quickly followed. The Slovenian courts had
overturned the final appeal by the campaigners that morning but
it seemed as if no-one had told the security staff that logging was
about to begin so soon and they were swamped by the swell of
protesters rushing towards them. Wolf watched Madja scampering
past the guards' line, filming her nimble escape into the obscurity

of the woods and the clumsy efforts of one of the guards to chase after her.

As the protesters surrounded the remaining security staff it seemed for a moment that they might overwhelm them, however, wooden clubs soon began to rise into the air and swing downwards in juddering arcs. Wolf drew back. Long and painful personal experience had taught him how dangerous such situations could become. He looked around for the ringleaders to tell them to move the protesters away from confrontation but when he spotted someone who was supposed to be marshalling the protest she was goading the guards and urging other protesters to attack them. The security guards were vicious in their response turning their clubs on anyone who got in their path. Wolf looked around to make sure that the television crews who had gathered were filming what was happening, before continuing with his own recording. It was a rout and most of the protesters, many of them bleeding, began to retreat but the fired-up security men kept chasing after them and Wolf recorded outright gang assaults on both men and women curled into protective balls as they lay on the ground.

'They are going to kill someone if they don't stop,' a woman said to him.

Wolf recognised Madja's partner, Alenka, and nodded his agreement.

'Maybe if someone is killed we will have a martyr and the recriminations will force the developers to stop work,' Alenka said.

Wolf was shocked not so much by her outrageous comment but because exactly the same thought had just passed through his own mind.

The security guard with his body armour and bulky weapons had quickly fallen behind and Madja was soon hidden by the trees. As she slipped deeper into the forest the sound of the battle receded and was replaced by whining chainsaws. Madja scouted closer to where the lumberjacks were working and was stunned by how much damage they had already done. They worked in teams with one man cutting down the oaks and others following behind to slice away the branches. The felled and stripped trunks were then wrapped in chains and dragged away by tractors. A large scar had already been cut into 10,000-year-old forest and the lumberjacks were moving towards where Madja crouched. She reached to the lower branches of the tree she was standing beside to haul herself up, determined to make a stand rather than be simply dragged away kicking and screaming.

Erik Dolar stood back as the oak began to tilt, its decent accompanied by an almost human like groan which grew louder until it crashed into the ground. Others began to strip at the branches and chains were pulled forward to haul the trunk away. Erik moved onto the next tree, mentally calculating the growing bonus he had earned that day. Their instructions had been clear, move in and clear as many trees as possible before nightfall in case there was some unexpected legal move by the protesters. Over the past two hours Erik and his co-workers had felled more than 100 trees. He looked at his watch and calculated there was at least another three hours of daylight, which in purely monetary terms would pay the deposit for a holiday with his wife and children to Italy that summer. Smiling with satisfaction he adjusted his ear muffs and moved on to the next target.

Wolf tightened a bandage around the head of a middle-aged woman. He'd had to cut off a patch of blood-matted hair before he could get to the wound and although he was able to staunch the bleeding he told the woman to make her way to a nearby hospital. In his younger days Wolf had been a distinctive figure dressed in jungle combats with dreadlocked hair but by his mid-thirties he reinvented himself and went to the other extreme by shaving it all off and dressing all in black. He became less of an action figure and more a commentator and green philosopher. The main vehicle for his opinions was the website ecopunks which he set up with a number of other activists and ran from his adopted home in Amsterdam. He was their star writer but its success was also down to an innovative design team who knew how to maximise the use of text, images, graphics, video clips and music to create an authoritative information source which also allowed regular visitors to affirm their alternative lifestyle.

Although his work on the ecopunks website meant that he now spent most of his time in Amsterdam an email from Madja had twigged his interest. He'd always had a soft spot for obscure campaigns which the larger environmental campaign groups tended to overlook. He also sensed in Madja a passion and a belief in the cause she was fighting for, which he had once shared but which it seemed in recent years had been replaced by a feeling that he was just doing a job.

Wolf's previous reputation ensured that his appearance at the protest camp gave it a major publicity boost as journalists, photographers and film crews arrived to report on the involvement of the German ecowarrior. However, although Wolf was happy to have his photo taken with the other protesters and to rhyme off a few soundbites he began to coach Madja on how to deal with the media. She was by nature quiet and timid and had always sat at the edge of groups and listened to what had been said, content to allow the more assertive Alenka speak for them both. Now for the first time she began to voice an opinion, articulating thoughts and ideas and being amazed that those around her took the trouble to listen and on occasions even nod in vigorous agreement.

She led the news headlines in Slovenia when she confronted a startled government minister by advising him that construction work on the proposed motorway could cause toxic bleeding into underground water channels that would impact on his hometown and its surrounding farmlands which made up his electoral powerbase. The minister was left blustering. Suddenly those who had seen the new road as simply a quicker means of getting to work in the morning began to doubt whether it was such a good idea.

Other countries started to take an interest as well. Slovenia was one of the most forested regions in Europe and had a unique ecosystem where the Alps and the Mediterranean came together. There seemed to be a stirring of collective guilt that it was now about to start destroying parts of its natural heritage for the sake of a few kilometres of motorway at a time when other more industrialised nations were wringing their hands in angst over the damage they had done to theirs. Green politicians and activists began to gather at the small camp of a dozen canvas shelters that had been established in the heart of the forest, right in the path of the first section which was due to be cleared.

'Are you satisfied with this little debacle?' demanded a gaunt looking man standing over Wolf as he worked on his laptop.

Wolf recognised him as Anton Feus, one of Slovenia's leading Green politicians who had spearheaded the legal battle to try and prevent the loggers starting work. It was obvious that Feus had made up his mind on what had happened but Wolf's antagonism to self-righteous lecturing was already ignited.

'How do you mean?' demanded Wolf, standing up.

'We have probably lost the support of the majority of people in this country who were behind the court campaign to stop the motorway,' retorted Feus.

'I thought the courts had backed the developers and that campaign was over. I didn't agree with the push to attack, there are more subtle ways of preventing the logging, but you saw the anger when people heard the chainsaws starting up it was entirely spontaneous,' said Wolf.

'Anger is fine but you pushed forward, the security guards will simply say they came under attack.'

'I didn't see any of the protesters armed with clubs and beating ten types of shite out of anyone who came near them.'

'Yes but you pushed first and they reacted ... overreacted sure but they will just say it was in self defence.'

'I didn't push anywhere. I've been battered around the head too many times in the past to do something like that.'

'So you just get others to do your dirty work for you now. Is that it?' exploded Feus.

Wolf walked away. Because of his profile and history of activism there was always a danger that he could become the fall guy. It had happened before and no amount of denial would help, especially when former allies began to side with the ranks of his accusers.

2

KEI YOSHIRO LEFT HER TENT AND walked the short distance to the excavation site where labourers were shoveling sand away from a stone entrance. The sandstorm had lasted only a couple of hours but in that time the surrounding landscape had shifted, new hillocks had formed while others had been sunk into stunted, smaller shapes. Kei imagined that it must be like having a long-term perspective on a mountain range where over millions of years once comfortingly familiar peaks are eroded away while seismic shifts beneath the surface of the planet force up new ones to redefine the horizon. Once again the opening into the stone structure had been cleared and the curving walls were exposed to daylight for six or seven metres on each side. The rest of the exterior lay beneath tonnes of ever-shifting sand. During the sandstorm Kei had warned the dig leader Mark Sheriff that unless more archaeologists were brought in it was only a matter of time until whole thing was buried once again beneath the Sahara. Mark had shrugged helplessly for the political situation in Mauritania was volatile and the government was more concerned with unrest and economic stagnation than unearthing its heritage.

Kei had moved to London six months earlier from her native Japan to try to lift herself out of the career rut and a general dissatisfaction with the direction her life had taken. She had worked with Mark, an archaeological expert on North Africa, on numerous digs before and contacted him on the off-chance that he might have some work available. Within an hour he wrote back telling her that had been asked by the Mauritanian ministry of culture to examine a site in the desert. The budget allocated to the dig was minimal and the site, one hundred kilometres from the nearest town with running water, was remote and difficult to get to. Despite the pathetic wage Kei had agreed to join him.

When Kei arrived the small team had already uncovered the entrance and found a passage sloping upwards towards a chamber. The passage chamber had been filled with sand but it did not take long to clear it and the three smaller chambers on either side. The layout was described in archaeological terms as cruciform – a long passage rose upwards leading to a central chamber, with ante-chambers to either side and one directly opposite the main entrance passage. There was also a narrow shaft dug into the roof which emerged just above the entrance.

As if the solid stone structure in the middle of the desert was not an enigma in itself, its contents provided enough material to keep the two archaeologists and their handful of student assistants from a Mauritanian university busy for years. The remains of various items had been found throughout the structure but decayed to such a point that several had disintegrated to dust upon being exposed to the fresh air. However, drawings and inscriptions chipped into the structure's ceiling and walls remained clearly visible once the residual sand had been carefully scraped away.

Kei found her feet sinking into the new layers of hot sand that had invaded the excavation site. The morning temperature was already above 100 degrees and rising and she stopped to take a breathless swig from her bottle of water and try to visualise the rest of the circular structure that lay beneath the desert. The site had been identified by Berbers who had passed through the area for generations and been totally unaware that anything other than sand had existed in this part of the desert. A vicious sandstorm two months earlier had created a huge crater more than 30 metres deep and around half a kilometre long and at the bottom of it a section of brickwork had been exposed.

Kei sighed with excitement and made her way towards the entrance and ducked into the welcoming shade. Inside she shone a torch at the ceiling. It was hard to make out exactly what the fine-line drawings were of, they seemed to suggest patterns and objects rather than simply depicting anything. Staring at them, Kei made out what she thought were human faces, animals, birds and trees. Other drawings seemed to show ships, blazing suns, rivers and constellations of stars but after gazing at them for a period of time they seemed to shift into the purely abstract, mocking any attempt to give them shape or form. There were other more formal patterns, series of lines and slashes that once again could seem purely random, but with the constant hint of some pattern. Kei made her way down the passage to where Mark was shuffling through a sheaf of papers.

'We need to get those mummies shifted soon in case there is another storm, at least if this place is buried completely we will have those to work on and the photos,' Kei said, nodding towards the side chamber where the bodies had been discovered.

'The government minister has said he wants to consult with religious leaders before he makes a decision,' Mark replied.

'So you keep telling me. What's that?' Kei demanded, nodding towards the papers.

Mark looked uncomfortable before motioning for her to move closer.

'Preliminary carbon dating of the mummies,' he whispered. 'But these can only be treated as unofficial until the minister gives us approval to examine them. I sent a few pieces of the bindings, bits of skin and tufts of hair to my wife at her laboratory in Cardiff and she ran them through.'

Mark looked about himself as Kei waited impatiently.

'And?' she demanded.

'The material is giving us an age of between 17,000 and 11,000 years, but there could be contamination,' Mark said.

'That's old. And what about the one with the red hair, did she identify what the dye was made off?'

Mark grimaced. 'It wasn't dyed,' he said. 'The corpse had natural red hair and according to the DNA was probably Caucasian. The other four are African, although Valerie hasn't ruled out the possibility of interbreeding in the smallest one which may have been a young adult.'

'If those dating results are right that would make them at least seven thousand years older than the Egyptian mummies,' said Kei.

'It's an unfortunate date,' sighed Sheriff. 'It opens up all sorts of opportunities for wild theories from your crank colleagues.'

Kei smiled aware of her colleague's antipathy to those who had become known as alternative historians, including herself, although years of friendship had made Mark slightly more indulgent towards her.

'A tall Caucasian, red head, mummified and buried in a sophisticated temple in an area of Africa that has probably been buried under the desert for at least 10,000 years,' she said to Mark.

'You have to admit that is a gift to the alternative history school of thought.'

'But we don't know that for sure,' countered Mark. 'There are a lot of possibilities. This particular area may not have been under sand for that entire period. Some areas may have survived desertification longer than others.'

'What about the carbon dating?' demanded Kei.

'It could have been corrupted, it was just a rough test, we can't be sure until we properly examine the mummies under laboratory conditions.'

Kei set about mapping the layout of the structure, taking measurements and photographs. She had studied ancient remains throughout North Africa, including those in Egypt, but had never come across anything like this. Yet there was something familiar about it and she wracked her brain to think of where she had seen a picture or read a description of something similar. The inscriptions on the walls bore no resemblance to the hieroglyphs associated with the pharaohs beyond the fact that they included the occasional bird or human form, but these were much more suggestive than the clear-cut outlines of ancient Egypt. She sat back and squinted at one trying to let the abstract shapes form into a pattern. Once again she thought she could make out a face, a boat on a river and an arrow, but then they seemed to dissolve into chaos. It was as if her eyes were playing tricks on her in the same way that she used to try and spot shapes in a drifting cloud. Another pattern caught her eye, a spiral that she briefly thought might represent the Milky Way. She smirked as she thought of Mark's face when she told him that. The alternative historians depended heavily on the fact that many ancient structures seemed to be based on an intimate knowledge of astronomy.

Suddenly Kei jumped from where she was crouched and hurried to where the narrow shaft in the roof emerged.

'Just like Newgrange,' she muttered to herself.

3

LORCAN O'MALLEY SAT PERFECTLY STILL WATCHING
the two salmon nestle close to one another on the river bed. The
male had seen off two competitors for the female's attention with
a combination of butting and biting and now with its new partner
began to nuzzle into the gravel to clear a space for her eggs for him
to fertilise. Lorcan had been sitting for three hours in anticipation
of the mating and dared not move to get a closer look in case he
startled the fish. He was staring with such concentration that he
failed to see a movement further along the bank or the sleek shadow
just below the surface of the gently flowing river. He jumped back
as the otter suddenly exploded from beneath the water with a silver
body writhing in its mouth. The animal pulled itself back onto the
bank of the river where with a yelp it briefly released and snapped
at the fish's head. Within a minute the otter had torn most of the
salmon's body apart and devoured it leaving just a stain of blood
and a few scales on the grass.

Lorcan watched dismayed as the otter scurried back towards its muddy slide and into the water from where it swam down stream. He had lived in the countryside long enough to realise that nature was essentially predatory and that slaughter and death happened every second, but the sight disturbed him, especially because the salmon was a species close to his heart. He edged his body over the river to where the two salmon had been nestling and pushed his arms into the water to ease a covering of gravel over the still visible indent in the river bed. He feared that most of the eggs and the male's semen would have been scattered by the recent commotion but perhaps one or two would fertilise and hatch. He presumed the male had been killed as it was closest to the otter when it struck. If that was so the female would still be in the area and if it avoided another attack it would come back to this pool to die – it's decaying body providing nutrients for the hatching salmon fry it had produced.

The life cycle of the salmon was evidence for Lorcan of a psychic backdrop to everyday reality – and on some occasions he might even concede it suggested a benign deity. The salmon that had just died would have spawned in this same pool four or five years earlier and begun to swim downstream when it was still a tiny smolt. As it came closer to the open sea its body had started to metamorphose and expand so that it could survive in salt water where it spent another couple of years swimming many hundreds of miles up to the coast of Norway to feed. Having survived the trials of the sea the salmon eventually would have felt an urge to return to its spawning ground. This was the really incredible part for Lorcan, for he had read that the fish could 'smell' the rivers of their birth and navigate their way home. He looked at the river and tried to conceive of it having a smell.

There was a Buddhist parable which compared the cycle of life and death and ultimate enlightenment to a river flowing into the ocean. The river was a metaphor for a soul reincarnating through the ages, never still and constantly changing its identity as it flowed from the mountains until it reached the sea where it suddenly stopped being a river and became part of a much vaster entity, its individuality subsumed. The parable suggested that this was the destiny of the human soul, to pass from the temporary egotistical illusion of separateness and achieve enlightenment by merging with a greater cosmic force. But coming from a western mindset Lorcan had found this uncomfortable to come to terms with – egotistical or not, he could not help seeing himself as an individual and the thought of his life experiences, and others from before that he only had a vague inkling of, being blanked out as he was absorbed by a cosmic ocean held as much comfort for him as the total negation of an atheist's death. But perhaps the myth could be resurrected for a western mind when taken in conjunction with the scientific belief that a river had a smell, discernible to its native salmon in the vastness of the ocean. Did that not suggest that the river retained some of its identity – a part of the Atlantic, yet retaining a semblance of its origin, still holding onto traces of once being the Owenbeg, the Bann or the Shannon? Surely the myth could now suggest that while the soul of Lorcan O'Malley might one day pass beyond the banks of its human incarnations into the ocean of enlightenment that he would retain his egotistical smell?

The idea excited him and he moved from where he sat, keen to return to his books and reread the Eastern texts that he had gathered and his collection of nature journals to try and develop this new theory. There were other references too that he was keen to follow up for the salmon had a unique place in Irish mythology. As he ambled down the mountain, already mentally locating the shelves and cupboards where he could find the books that he would need and planning out his day until with a start he remembered that he was also responsible for looking after his granddaughter Irinda. It was an idea he was still getting used to. He looked at the rising sun and estimated that it must now be nearly 7am and that Irinda would soon be awakening. He hurried over the rough hilly ground and cut through a forest of yews to the small plot of land where he had built his house, mostly from the tumbled bricks of the previous dwelling that had stood there.

4

THE BATTERED ENVIRONMENTAL PROTESTERS stood in subdued groups as the growl of chainsaws and groan of tumbling trees crashing to the ground continued unabated. Wolf worked at his laptop, emailing a report and film footage of that afternoon's events to Niels in Amsterdam to be posted on the ecopunks website. Wolf had scanned a number of online mainstream news channels and the events in Slovenia were topping the agenda. However, all the reports accused the protesters of instigating the violence. The video footage tended to focus on protesters goading the security guards and hurling stones and bottles at them and while there was footage of guards batoning the protesters it did not illustrate the intensity of those attacks. Anton Feus had distanced himself from the events, accusing outsiders, although he did not mention any names, of coming in and hijacking what had been a peaceful campaign. No-one else named him either but all the reports included pictures of Wolf with one or two carrying profiles of the 'notorious German ecoterrorist'.

For a few days he had really believed that the protest in the forest might have been successful. A number of countries had expressed concern and there had been anxious rumblings among members of the Slovenian government. The symbolism of the victory would have been as important as the preservation of the forest itself for it would have set a precedent that other states would have found difficult to ignore. Now there was no mention of the issue that had been at the heart of the protest. Just reports about the violence.

Wolf wondered why he still took such defeats so personally. He had achieved what appeared to be numerous successes but knew that inevitably many campaigns he had been involved in had ultimately ended in failure. He had helped stop drilling projects in Alaska, shipments of nuclear waste in Europe and tree felling in the Amazonian jungle, but often these had simply been stays of execution and months or years after the publicity had died down the drillers, nuclear reprocessors and loggers had simply gone ahead when no-one was looking.

Alenka came towards him, agitated and clutching a mobile phone.

'We have to stop them,' she shouted. 'Madja can't get down.'

Wolf was startled from his contemplation and looked at her confused.

'Where is she?' he asked.

'They can't hear her and she can't get down from the tree. She just phoned me, she thinks she is going to die.'

'Call her,' said Wolf, a mental picture of what was happening in the forest forming.

Alenka dialled and handed her phone to Wolf. However, when the call was answered the noise of destruction from the other end was even more intense.

'Hurry Alenka,' cried the voice at the other end. 'They are getting closer, I can't move.'

'It's Wolf,' he shouted into the phone.

He could not hear what Alenka said back and was not even sure that she had heard him above all the din.

'Have you still got your coat on?' he shouted. 'Try waving it to draw attention.'

'Hurry up and stop them,' wailed Madja.

Wolf shut down his laptop and handed it to Alenka before moving towards the line of security guards. They stiffened as he approached and tightened their grip on their batons. The despondent protesters began buzzing as they became aware that something was happening and cheered as they saw Wolf moving forward although they held back from following him. One of the security guards stepped forward from the line to halt Wolf's progress, putting an arm out to stop him. He was helmetted and swathed in heavy black body armour and looked to be an impenetrable block in the path of the gangly, bald activist.

'There is a girl in one of the trees and the loggers are about to cut it down,' Wolf said.

The guard shrugged, he had expected physical confrontation rather than being forced to deal with information.

'She shouldn't be in there,' he said.

'Maybe not, but she is and unless you do something she will be killed.'

Wolf thrust the mobile phone towards the guard and he took it without thinking.

'You can talk to her if you want,' he said.

The guard shuffled uncomfortably, regretting his decision to come forward to face the intruder. His instructions were simple, to keep protesters out of the forest, not to engage in conversation with them. He had simply moved forward because it seemed as if Wolf had been making a beeline towards him. He looked at the phone in one hand and baton in the other and wondered what to do. He did not disbelieve Wolf, he had seen people break through their lines during the initial push forward by the protesters and three had been caught, but if one of them was in a tree he did not see that this was his problem.

'I will try and get a message to someone,' he said reluctantly.

Wolf looked at the guard doubtfully.

'OK, thanks. Please do it now, though.'

Wolf turned and began to walk away from the line of security guards and stopped suddenly and began to absentmindedly pat his pockets. When he turned to look back the guard he had been talking to was back at his line and three or four other guards had come towards him to find out what had been said.

'My phone,' called Wolf, and turned back towards the guards.

The small group stiffened again as he approached, but when the man who had been talking to Wolf turned and held out the phone towards him the tension among the others eased and they lowered their batons. Suddenly when he was just a few steps from the cluster of security guards and reaching for the phone Wolf darted to the right and pushed one of them aside before sprinting towards forest. The group stood stunned at the sudden movement and Wolf was already hidden by the trees when they let out a collective roar and turned to move after him. As before their body armour made it difficult for them to manoeuvre between the trees and the thick gnarled roots that twisted along the forest floor. Wolf had gone just far enough into the forest to be out of sight before grabbing a branch and hauling himself above the ground and crouching on a sturdy bough close to the tree trunk. Seconds later three of the guards crashed past below, pushing aimlessly through the dense foliage in search of him. Wolf waited until they had passed before lowering himself to the ground and moving slowly towards the noise of the chainsaws. His body was tense and he was alert to every movement, sprawling on the ground when he saw one of the guards randomly slashing at a patch of undergrowth before moving on. Wolf had no firm plan, he simply hoped to get to where the loggers were working and try to spot Madja's coat among the trees and either help her down or point her out to the security guards, although he suspected they would swoop on him before he even got time to raise a finger.

Madja sobbed as she saw another tree crash on to the ground and the loggers move even closer towards her. A huge clearing running for several hundred metres had opened up and the tree to which she clung was now in the front line. There were at least a dozen teams of loggers working and their ruthless efficiency meant that it could only be a matter of minutes until they reached her. She had tried to do as Wolf had suggested and removed her blue anorak to wave and try to attract attention, but she was paralysed and dared not let go her grip on the tree trunk. Her voice was hoarse and she could no longer scream for help. She tried to manoeuvre her mobile phone again and try to make another call. As well as Alenka she had phoned the police and her parents but the noise around her made it difficult to hear what they had said and if they had even acknowledge the perilous situation in which she was. Clumsily she tried to dial her parent's number again without loosening her grip on the tree trunk but as soon as she saw that the call had been connected and tried to move the phone to her ear she lost her grip and it dropped through the branches and out of sight towards the forest floor. Despite her raw-worn throat Madja let out a piercing scream of despair.

Wolf started as he half heard the cry. Despite the mechanical din made by the loggers and the tractors dragging the felled trees away to be branched Madja's primal wail had given him a general direction in which to focus his search. The clearing in the forest meant that he had an uninterrupted view to where the loggers were working and he thought he saw a flash of blue in one of the trees. Trusting to fate, Wolf broke cover and started running at a careful lop to ensure that is feet did not get caught in the tangled mess of roots and foliage that still covered the clearing. He heard a shout from behind him and was aware of the guards coming after him and then, more alarmingly, the sound of a gun being fired and a bullet slicing the air above his head. He was close to the tree where he thought he had seen Madja's blue coat and where a logger had already made his first cut. He looked up but could see nothing and by the time he had returned his concentration to the ground it was too late to avoid the tendril of exposed root which caught his left foot and sent him sprawling.

Erik Dolar was tiring from the day's work and sighed as he moved on to another oak. His arms were throbbing from holding the heavy chainsaw and his shoulders were clenched into a knot of tension from the constant vibration of the metal teeth on wood. Suddenly among the snow of sawdust falling to the ground he noticed a lurid yellow object with an LCD screen flashing. He was so stunned by the unexpected find that he lowered his chainsaw and left it running on standby as he reached to lift it.

He stood up straight and wondered whether he should answer the call or not but before he came to a decision he heard a commotion behind him and when he turned he saw a lank figure dressed in black running towards him. Behind the bald man he saw three security guards chasing him. One of them stopped to raise a rifle and take aim at the running figure, but just as he fired the man in black seemed to dive towards the ground and Erik felt as if he had been punched in the chest. He staggered backwards in shock against the tree which he had been working and then slumped as a searing pain spread across his torso before blacking out.

5

THE DAWN SKY ABOVE EGYPT BRIGHTENED from black to blue and the horizon turned bright orange on March 20th 10500 BC. It was the spring equinox, when night and day were exactly the same length. On the horizon the stars that made up the constellation of Leo faded from view as the sun rose in front of them. Facing east towards the rising sun was the huge lion-shaped sculpture which many millennia later would be known as The Sphinx. Suddenly it was night again and the sky began to move in quick-time as centuries were compressed into seconds and there was a discernible shift in where stars and constellations lay. The constellation of Leo edged away from the point of sunrise during the spring equinox and was replaced by Cancer, then Gemini, then Taurus, then Aries and finally Pisces which by the start of the 21st Century was being edged out of place by the constellation of Aquarius.

Kei called up the settings for the graphic display she was running on her laptop and keyed in the geographic co-ordinates of her current location. The programme could display the night sky on any particular part of the planet during any period of history – past or still to come. It was a favoured method of the alternative historians for linking man-made objects with the stars in the night sky. Because of a process known as precession, whereby the earth wobbled around its own axis over a 26,000 year period, the positions of stars and constellations appeared to change in relation to where the sun rose and set. This meant that whereas the sun had appeared to rise at a point on the horizon where the constellation of Leo had just been during the spring equinox of around 12,500 years ago, each of the 12 constellations of the Zodiac would appear at this point as the centuries passed by and occupy it at sunrise for approximately 2,200 years.

The theory was that because the Sphinx was facing the exact point on the horizon where the sun rose and was carved in the shape of a lion it was reasonable to assume that it was associated with Leo, the astrological symbol for the lion. This ran in the face of conventional historians who argued that the Sphinx was build around 3,000 BC. However, in that period of history the sun would have risen on March 20th in front of the constellation of Taurus. The alternative historians claimed in that case a more obvious animal to base the Sphinx on would have been a bull rather than a lion. Mainstream historians dismissed that outright, not least because all the conventional data pinpointed the first civilizations to around 8000BC, when humans were just starting to form primitive settled communities, two and a half millennia after their alternative counterparts were claiming that skilled craftsmen had carved the huge iconic figure and had a fairly sophisticated understanding of astronomy.

Kei glanced at her notebook where she had jotted down a reading from her compass and used school maths to calculate the angle of the shaft which ran from above the entrance of the desert structure into the central chamber. She then created a graphic on her laptop which would show the sky from the point of view of the chamber and started to run the programme to see what appeared there, however, she was quickly stumped. For a start the shaft was not east facing, but rather looked towards the north which meant that at no point during the day would the sun shine directly in it. She had been reminded of a similar shaft in the megalithic passage tomb at Newgrange in Ireland which was angled in such a way that on the winter solstice – the shortest day of the year – the first rays of the rising sun shone through it directly into its central chamber, gradually lighting it up. But for this to happen in the desert structure the shaft would have had to be facing east. Kei focused on the signs of the Zodiac, which had an ancient mythical status in countries throughout the world, but while the constellations and majors stars appeared within view at various times there was nothing remarkable about those times. She checked the morning and evening skies during the spring and autumn equinoxes as well as the winter and summer solstices for the entire 24,000-year precessional cycle but drew a complete blank.

'That doesn't make sense,' she muttered to herself.

'What doesn't?' demanded Mark who had just come in.

'The shaft,' replied Kei. 'It appears to be just pointing at a random point in the sky. I mean what is the point of that, surely it should be aimed at something, sunset or sunrise or whatever, but it is pointing north.'

'What about Polaris?' asked Mark.

'No. In 10500 BC Polaris would have been to the right of the line of vision from the catafalque through the shaft. Given the effects of precession its position would have varied over the millennia but there is never any direct alignment with it nor any of the major stars or constellations during any period of history at either sunset or sunrise.

'Why do you keep coming back to 10500BC? I never quite got that,' sighed Mark.

Kei smiled at his expression.

'The alternative historians have hit on it as the time when some great catastrophe took place and destroyed an advanced civilization that existed then,' she said.

'Please don't say Atlantis.'

'Not necessarily but I think there are plenty who have tried to tag that on to what is controversial but fairly well documented research. The theme of some sort of devastating flood has been stored in the folk memory of many traditions.'

'Such as?' said Mark.

'Well in Judaism and Christianity there is the story of Noah building an ark to escape the devastation of the flood that wiped out human civilization. There are similar myths from every continent, so presumably they all relate to some event in history.'

'But that doesn't necessarily have to mean they are all based on the same event,' said Mark. 'Let's face it we know that volcanic activity and earthquakes were responsible for causing tsunamis all over the world and that tide levels have fallen and risen over the millennia as ice caps formed and melted, so sure I can accept that survivors of such a disaster would hand down such stories to their descendants and that in time these would become part of an oral storytelling tradition and even transformed into creation myths and tales of vengeful gods, but don't tell me that they all happened at exactly the same time.'

'Well why not?' retorted Kei, not so much because she was totally convinced by the theory herself but because she wanted to test the argument. 'We know that the last global ice age ended between

14000 and 10000 BC and that huge ice sheets covered most of northern Europe, including what is now your plush little hideaway in Wales. Now the ice sheets would have locked up huge volumes of water that when they began to melt would have caused sea levels to rise and would have destroyed the coastal settlements of humans. I mean the release of all that water would have had a global impact.'

'I agree and there is sound archaeological evidence to prove that but what we do not have is evidence to show that this all happened overnight. It would have happened over centuries, and sure there would come a day when people living in a coastal area would come to the realisation that they must move because their homes were being swamped by the sea, but it didn't all happen in an instant.'

'But there is evidence all around the Mediterranean that cities and communities were submerged because of sudden rises in the sea levels and that pattern is repeated across the world. I have dived at underwater sites off the coast of Japan,' said Kei.

'Yes but all those sites fall in with the conventional timeline which asserts that the first human civilizations began appearing around 8000BC. Nothing has been found to date a human civilization before that date.'

'But that is where the theory of total, sudden and absolute disaster comes in – a global event so powerful that all traces of whatever human civilization that existed at that time were completely destroyed,' said Kei. 'Just think of the implications if something like that did happen. Why is it so impossible that there was an ancient civilization that was wiped out by some natural disaster. It doesn't even take anything as radical as that to end a civilization. Roman civilization rose and fell over 1,200 years and in its time included great architecture, culture and philosophy, yet it eventually collapsed. Why can you not consider the possibility that in the tens of thousands of years of human history at a much earlier point than generally accepted there was a fairly sophisticated civilization that because of some disaster was wiped out.'

'But there is no hardcore evidence,' Mark said. 'I mean it is all very well for you and your alternative colleagues to speculate on a 12,000 year old global civilization stretching from Angkor Wat in Cambodia to Tiahuanaco in Bolivia and the pyramids of Egypt and Mexico but none of those sites dates back more than 5,000 years which is well within the realms of conventional theories about history.'

'Well no-one has ever said that they are part of the same civilization,' said Kei. 'But we are saying is that those structures you mentioned all show sophisticated building techniques that seemed to be based on astronomical alignments. The suggestion is not that they date back to 12,000 years ago or more but that the technology used to build them was out of sync with other more common and primitive structures at the time and that they seem to reflect astronomical alignments which would only correspond with the view of the night sky in around 10500BC rather than the era in which they were built.'

'I've read that as well and it has been challenged. They say the pyramids in Egypt are supposed to mirror Orion, the layout of Angkor Wat is somehow linked to the constellation of Draco and Tihuanaco is aligned to the equinoxes. But it all involves convoluted maths and turning things upside down to make the theory fit … and even if they were all true what is the link between Draco, Orion and sunrise on March 21 every year anyway.'

'I don't know,' admitted Kei. 'Yes, the maths can be convoluted but it exists. Maybe we are trying to find patterns were none exist or are just looking at the wrong patterns. What I am saying is you don't have to buy in to one person's pet theory, but that also goes for the more traditional schools of thought which tend to dismiss alignments and similarities between the stonework and layouts of different structures separated by thousands of miles and huge oceans as mere coincidence.'

'So if you are not saying that those diverse sites were not part of a single civilization what are you saying?'

'That there was a common source. The earlier civilization would not necessarily have been confined to one region – it could well have been global, but communicating and sharing ideas and technology. Following the disaster a few survivors would have been left and it was they and their descendants who preserved the technology, roaming the earth and helping to kick start later civilizations.'

6

LORCAN'S NEIGHBOUR BRIDGEEN HANNA, FROM whom he had brought the plot of land on which the house was built, was dozing in the armchair beside the fire. She had been pleased when he asked her to babysit, although slightly taken aback when he asked her to come at 4 o-clock in the morning, but then having lived close to Lorcan for several years now she was used to his irregular hours and eccentricities.

'Did you get what you were looking for?' she said, jumping awake as Lorcan came in through the front door.

'No not really,' Lorcan said, looking towards the room where Irinda was.

'She's still sleeping. My daughter is leaving her children over later. If you want I can send them over to fetch the little one and they can play for a while.'

Lorcan beamed at Bridgeen's kindness.

'Yes, That would be good. I think she needs company ... and some TV. I don't think she can comprehend that someone can live without the thing.'

'Mr O'Malley, most people in this day and age can't comprehend why someone in a civilized country would choose to live without electricity, but it doesn't seem to bother you.'

'No need for it. Sure a good stack of turf and driftwood keeps the house warm and heats the pots, and candles give me plenty of light to read by. What do I need that stuff for?'

Bridgeen sighed helplessly as she left and looked at Lorcan with the impression she kept coming back to that despite all his books and learned ways her neighbour was a bit soft in the head.

Lorcan poked the fire into life to boil up a pot of water to make some tea and then some stock for soup later on. A fresh basket of vegetables, pulled from his garden by himself and Irinda the previous day, sat on the kitchen table and he began to wash these and cut them into bite-sized chunks.

He was a man in his sixties with deep-set eyes and white hair that seemed to cascade from his head. For much of his life he had worked as a government employee in a huge area of mountain bogland in the west of Ireland where he repaired pathways, logged plant, insect, bird and animal species, and kept an eye on the herds of wild goats that roamed it. He had been lucky to get such a job where he could spend his days outdoors and in solitude, because cities and people had come to terrify him. Before, what he had come to regard as his estrangement from society, he'd had a modestly successful career as a folk musician, playing mandolin with a traditional group and touring Europe. He had lived a carefree and bohemian existence until his mind had tipped into a reality which he suspected ran at a tangent from the rest of humanity. His entire being had been scorched and left frazzled and he felt unable to cope with society. Vivid images would explode in his skull and leave him reeling as he walked through a city street – it was only in the countryside that he felt able to come to terms with the demons that plagued him. An old friend, with whom he had once played in a group, was a manager in the government department with responsibility for Ireland's natural heritage. He had helped Lorcan to return home and it was through him that he secured his post. A small cottage came with the job and he was able to live isolated from society, avoiding contact with people for weeks at a time, while earning enough money to keep himself fed and to send off for the books that he felt he needed in order to come to terms with what had happened to him. He spent more than a third of a century living the life of an almost total recluse on the side of the mountain, reading mystical texts from India, the Far East and Europe and slowly accepting that perhaps his mind had been opened in a way that few others had and that he should allow the visions that came to him to play out and try to come to terms with them. He could never accept what had happened to him but at least he was better able to live with it, although he was still wary of society, which from what he had gleaned had become even more scary since his self-imposed exile.

Then about around four years ago one of the managers who occasionally called to check on his work and draw up a new schedule said Lorcan's name had been mentioned a couple of times on the radio and that there was an appeal for him to get in touch. Immediately Lorcan felt the demons of paranoia stirring, however, his manager said it had something to do with a piece of music he had recorded. Lorcan was curious and agreed to go with him to the main office and phone the radio station. Without him understanding exactly what they were talking about an excited producer told him that a piece of music he had written and recorded, called Mactíre, had been sampled by a British DJ and that the record had become a huge global success.

Lorcan reluctantly agreed to go on air and talk about the piece which he could barely remember and tell a few anecdotes about his brief musical career. He caused a bit of a stir for a few weeks and was featured in various newspapers, magazines and a few television news reports as a forgotten folk music pioneer who now lived as a mystic and a recluse. He quickly became reforgotten but in the wake of the publicity the record company of the artist who had sampled Mactíre wrote to him and offered to pay him royalties for use of the tune. The cheque was enough to allow Lorcan to resign his job, which he loved but whose routine he had come to resent. It also enabled him to buy a plot of land a mile from the coast and build his own cottage. There were several other major surprises for him for just a year ago a letter had arrived, forwarded from his previous address, telling him that he had a granddaughter. This came as a particular shock, for up to that point Lorcan hadn't even known that he'd had any children.

7

WOLF CURSED AS THE EXPOSED ROOT caught his foot and sent him tumbling to the ground, however, at the same time as he tripped he heard another shot ringing out. In his winded confusion he was unsure if the sudden searing pain running up his side had been caused by a bullet of if he had fallen on something. He had little time to contemplate it for suddenly he felt himself being dragged roughly to his feet and then punched in the face. He staggered back and crumpled to his knees and tried to curl himself into a protective ball in expectation of a full-blown assault. But hands began to grab him again and haul him to his feet. One of the armoured guards was screaming insults but was being held back by some of his colleagues. Wolf was still wary and his eyes darted all about him in full expectation of another attack but although he was still being gripped on either side by two guards his assailant was also being restrained. He looked down at his torso and could see no obvious wound, although his side was still painful. Wolf remembered the girl he had come to rescue. His heart sank as he saw a number of people gathered around a body that lay strewn upon the ground and covered in a blue anorak. Someone was trying to administer mouth-to-mouth resuscitation.

'Is she badly hurt?' Wolf demanded.

The guards holding him looked confused and Wolf realised he had reverted to his native German. He tried to ask the same question in pigeon Slovenian.

'The girl is fine but one of the lumberjacks has been shot,' muttered one of his captors. 'You should not talk.'

Wolf did not have to guess too hard who had shot the man as he saw a look that combined hatred and anxiety in the eyes of the guard who had attacked him.

'The police are here now,' one captor said to the other.

The attempts at reviving the logger were beginning to flag and the two guards who were holding Wolf began to push him towards the approaching policemen and away from their distraught colleague. Wolf did not resist. The security guards and the police spoke to one another in Slovenian that was way beyond the few simple phrases that Wolf had managed to teach himself. He suspected that beyond trespass there was little that he could be arrested for but given the increasingly agitated noises coming from the security guard who had fired the shot Wolf decided to put off any protest and allow himself to be taken from the site. From where he stood he could see the still body of Erik Dolar, his face now covered with Madja's anorak, but with a splash of blood clearly visible on his chest. Wolf had every sympathy for the dead man and the security guard who had shot him, but there was still the cold realisation that the bullet had had been meant for him.

When Madja has seen Erik reeling back from the force of the bullet her fear had evaporated and she slithered from the branch to which

46

she had been clinging for more than three hours and instinctively let her feet guide her to the ground. Blood was bubbling from Erik's chest and his breathing was already laboured. Madja pulled off her coat and laid it over the lumberjack's torso and turned to where she had seen Wolf fall, she was sure he had also been shot and was shocked to see him being dragged to his feet by one of the security men, a rifle swinging at his side, who punched Wolf full in the face before being pulled back by his colleagues. Erik was moaning and his eyes flickered open, staring straight ahead of him. Madja called for someone to come and help before bending over Erik and trying to sooth him. He seemed to respond as his eyes focused on her but then they softened before becoming fixed on some interminable point. Some of the other lumberjacks had arrived and one of them tried to shake Erik awake. Madja stared helplessly as she watched the logger trying vainly to revive his dead colleague.

When the police came Madja was handcuffed and taken to a van parked on a nearby country road where Wolf had already been placed. He looked drawn and wary, but smiled at Madja as she sat down beside him. Two policemen, armed with carbines, clambered into the van and sat at the door which was pushed closed and locked from the outside.

'Are you OK?' Wolf asked as the van's engine started.

'I'm sorry for getting you into all this trouble,' replied Madja. 'I just couldn't move and thought that I was going to die when the tree was cut down. I feel stupid because when that poor man was shot I was able to climb down in no time. Why couldn't I have done that earlier and stopped all this.'

Wolf nodded vaguely but could not think of anything so say that would comfort the girl. In the past three years he had been involved in incidents where six people had died. He could rationalise to himself that none of those deaths had been caused by him or resulted directly from his actions, but he had been there and been involved in the situation. Each time, as during that afternoon, it was only by some quirk of fate that he had survived and just a slight change of circumstances could have left him dead instead of someone else.

The police van started and began to trundle along a forest track until they felt it connect with a more solid surface and begin to speed up. Outside they could hear the sound of motorbikes and sirens and Wolf could visualise the vehicle in which he was travelling speeding along in a small convoy flanked by the outriders. He could only smile at the thought that any of the environmental groups to which he was affiliated could even contemplate trying to spring him from captivity, never mind actually pull off such an operation. Although he had never advocated physical violence he had often been branded a terrorist, usually by the corporations whose activity he was trying to disrupt or by the governments who supported them. The resistance he had participated in had been physical in the sense that it was his own body that he used to block convoys, trains or ships carrying toxic waste or, as in the case of the French government's activities in the Pacific Ocean, nuclear testing. He had suffered numerous batterings due to the positions he placed himself in and had been physically assaulted by a variety of police, army and private security guards after being dragged away from the media spotlight. Despite this it was he who was labelled the terrorist and he suspected that the death of Erik Dolar that afternoon would give fresh ammunition to those who chose to brand him in such a way. What concerned him was not so much the charges that the Slovenian authorities might be able to bring against him but the negative way in which his actions would be portrayed. In a broad sense it would damage the campaign to prevent the oak forest from being destroyed and Wolf knew from past experience that in the couple of days it would take for the media frenzy to die down and the basic facts to emerge that the logging company would have finished their task and moved onto their next target. However, there were other implications, for Wolf felt that his personal safety could now be at risk.

'I've never been arrested before,' sighed Madja.

'Its almost become a way of life for me,' mused Wolf.

'How many times? More than 100?'

'I'm not sure. My mum used to keep count.'

'Why did she stop?'

'She died from cancer about 20 years ago and she'd had it for more than 15 years before that from when I was just a kid. Mild treatable forms would come and go but then she started to develop more serious types. She kept battling but there always seemed to be an inevitability that it would take her in the end.'

'That must have been awful for her and you.'

'We lived close to Bonn where there is a nuclear power plant and trains carrying waste used to pass close by our apartment. She was always involved in protests – I can't be sure that mum would not have developed cancer anyway but it was always in her head that living so close to the railway was a factor. I hadn't really bothered with protests before that – I used to just think that was mum's thing, but when the cancer became terminal I started to look around for something to blame and hit out at.'

'That's understandable,' said Madja.

'Mum's protests had always been peaceful but I thought for all her hippy ideals she hadn't actually achieved anything, so I thought lets take this a stage further and I would steal cars and lorries and try to block the tracks and hurl myself at the police lines which were set up to guard the trains when they were forced to stop. That's when I started to get arrested. Mum was horrified and couldn't understand why I would want to harm another human being, even if they were guarding the trains.'

'Were you a violent person?'

'Angry and frustrated so I suppose that came out as physical aggression but then the only thing I had in the world was slipping away from because of these trains and their cargoes – or at least in my own mind they were to blame.'

'Do you not think that is true any more?'

'There is no hard evidence, or at least no-one has ever been able to produce any evidence. Three or four kids in my year at school, which was also near the railway line, all developed cancer and died. In the block of flats were we lived there seemed to be cancer sufferers on every floor. There were half a dozen blocks of flats beside the railway lines but the cancer seemed to cluster among the people whose apartments looked onto the railway tracks. We highlighted this to the government and they came out with Geiger counters and took blood tests but concluded it was a coincidence. They said similar clusters developed in other parts of the city which were nowhere near the railway lines or even the nuclear power station.'

'Do you believe them?'

'We were told that the carriages which carried the nuclear waste past our houses were sealed and that nothing could escape and that no-one could produce any evidence that these cargos were causing the cancer. Apart from the cancer cluster. No-one was ever able to explain that – they just waved their Geiger counters and pointed to academic surveys and government reports. Pure coincidence we were told. Maybe it was but after mum died and I got more involved it became less of a local issue for me and I began to look at the broader picture. Nuclear radiation kills – it causes cancer. Look at Chernobyl, Hiroshima and Nagasaki. The waste that nuclear reactors produce will be a danger to humanity for thousands of years to come.'

'Did you stay in Bonn?'

'No I had no other family. Mum was an only child and her parents were dead. I had friends and I still go to see them when I can, but I felt no real connection to the city.'

'Was your father not about?'

'I've never met him formally although I know where he lives, I even went to see him and spoke briefly to him but didn't tell him who I was.'

'That must have been a bit weird ... were you not tempted to say something to him and tell him who you were?'

'No. He never bothered with us so I didn't see why I should bother with him although after mum died it was hard not to make contact with him if for no other reason than to tell him what a complete cunt he was for abandoning mum and me.'

Madja looked startled at the venom with which Wolf spoke.

8

KEI SAT IN THE BACK OF an army truck with Mark surrounded by half a dozen heavily armed Mauritanian soldiers. They had come in the middle of the night and woken them with the sound of revving engines and spotlights shinning onto their desert camp. One of them told Kei that they had to pack up immediately as they were being evacuated from the dig. Kei looked to Mark, hoping that he would protest but it was plain that he was terrified and Kei was aware that any protests from an Asian woman in the middle of a north African desert would be contemptuously ignored.

'They must have found out that I sent that material to Wales for analysis before the culture minister gave his permission,' Mark whispered.

'But they asked you to come here in the first place,' Kei said, trying to sound soothing but conscious that her own voice was nervously shrill. Mark just shook his head and tensed as a lanky sergeant approached.

'Sorry about all this,' he said in perfectly clipped public school

English. 'Our Met people have forecast high winds in this area over the next few days and the minister has ordered us to evacuate you from here immediately.'

'What about the finds which are still inside the structure, can we take them?' asked Kei, looking to Mark for support.

'I have been told to facilitate you in any way and to make sure that you have time to gather as much as of your equipment as possible but nothing is to removed from the tomb,' the sergeant said apologetically.

'We are not sure that it is a tomb,' said Kei.

'Kei,' Mark growled. 'Leave it.'

'Hopefully you will be able to return when the storm has passed,' the sergeant said.

'But if the whole thing is buried again it will be lost to us,' Kei said.

'We will all be lost if we wait for too long,' the soldier said.

It did not take long for Kei and Mark and the other members of the dig team to pack their equipment and personal luggage while the soldiers quickly dismantled the camp before bundling them all into the back of the truck. They drove for several hours, bouncing over desert before they came to a town where they were checked into a small hotel. Kei was convinced that the storm was simply an excuse to get them off the dig site, however, when she woke in the morning she could hear a wind whipping itself into a frenzy and when she looked outside could see nothing but swirling sand.

She went down stairs to try to get breakfast and find Mark, who she was surprised to see dinning with the sergeant from the night before. The soldier stood as she approached and pulled out a chair to allow her to sit down.

'It doesn't look good, I'm afraid,' he said, surprising Kei once again with his clipped English.

'What did you hear?' Kei asked.

'The area were you were working has been badly hit. The sands are constantly shifting and it will now be unrecognisable,' he said. 'That would normally mean nothing as no-one lives there and the nomads who pass through know how to protect themselves but I can understand that it must be upsetting after all the work you carried out.'

'Well as you said, no-one lives there, so hopefully no-one was hurt.'

The sergeant smiled sadly.

'We are fortunate now that we have satellites and forecasters and can take such precautions, unfortunately that is not much use in the longer term,' he said. 'The Sahara Desert is a hungry beast and is constantly gobbling up once fertile land and forcing people to abandon their villages. Perhaps were you were digging was also once the home to a community that was swallowed up by the sands a long time ago?'

Mark nodded cautiously.

'It was a unique find,' he said. 'You said you could see the storm coming because of satellite images. Do you think is possible that your government would be able to pinpoint the site we were working again, using the same technology?'

'Undoubtedly, that is how we managed to find you, but I think the main issue for you now would be how to shift the tonnes of sand that have now probably filled in the huge hole in which you were working. You could not get machinery there and it would take a lot of digging by hand. Can you tell me what you found?'

Kei didn't look at Mark as she answered.

'Mummies,' she said.

The soldier looked startled.

'Like those in Egypt?' he asked.

'Same principle,' said Kei. 'Though the strange thing was one of them seemed to have red hair and we suspect may have been Caucasian and very very old.'

'We can't be sure,' Mark said, glaring at Kei. 'We were waiting for permission to carry out proper tests.'

'Its not that unusual,' Kei insisted, flicking through notes she had made. 'Mummies have been found all over the world and some have been dated 8,000 years old.'

'And do you think that one of the mummies you found here in Mauritania was Caucasian?' asked the soldier.

Kei could sense Mark shifting uncomfortable beside her.

'We can't be sure,' she replied cautiously. 'It had red hair and a lighter skin pigmentation.'

'There are rumours that Caucasians often came to this part of Africa and settled here. Some say that the Berbers are descended from them after they intermarried with black Africans and Arabs' the sergeant said.

'It worked both ways,' said Kei. 'There is evidence that Africans – or rather people with African features known as Olmecs – may have voyaged to Central America thousands of years before the Spanish conquistadores. In modern day Mexico there are huge stone carvings measuring up to two metres and weighing several tonnes that appear to depict human heads with what are described as negroid features. I have some pictures.'

Kei rummaged through the sheaf of internet printouts she kept among her notes and drew out a couple of pictures which she put on the table. The sergeant agreed that the carvings looked as if they had been modelled on the features of an African but Mark remained silent.

'The Olmecs are believed to be the ancestors of later cultures in Central America – including the Mayans and Aztecs – it could be that the Olmec carved these heads to honour a powerful people who moved among them or had taught them for they are found at sites that seem to have a religious connotation that sometimes even include pyramids. It is possible that the carved head predate the Mayan and Aztec aspects of these sites and are thousands of years older.'

'But that is nonsense,' sighed Mark.

The sergeant looked surprised at his outburst.

'Why?' he demanded. 'Why shouldn't Africans have travelled to other parts of the world. You are a black man who comes from England.'

'Wales,' corrected Kei.

'Whatever. My point is that humans have always migrated and are still doing so.'

'But the theory that Kei is putting forward is that humans were migrating across the planet and transmitting ideas to one another thousands of years before conventional history suggests,' said Mark.

'Well why not? Human beings are a migratory species,' said Kei. 'I mean conventional historians suggest that Aborigines ended up in Australia between 40,000 and 70,000 years ago, so clearly so-called primitive people managed to navigate around the globe. The generally accepted version of human evolution is that hominoids evolved in east Africa in what is modern day Ethiopia. The process took hundreds of thousands of years and there may were various subs species such as the Neanderthals who lived alongside homo sapiens and spread out into Asia and Europe before becoming extinct or else became subsumed into the more successful species that became modern man. We are still finding sub species. It was only recently that scientists found the skulls of tiny humans in Bali, who they nicknamed as hobbits. They were believed to have died out just 13,000 years ago which is not that long in terms of human history.'

'So what is the point you are making?' demanded Mark.

'Simply that if with all the science we have at our disposal we are still only finding evidence of an entire human-like species that until recently we knew nothing about why is it so unreasonable to assume that there were earlier civilizations pre-dating the ones we know about?'

9

LORCAN STRODE DOWN THE HILL FROM his house and cut through a field, scattering grazing sheep, until he came to Bridgeen's house. As usual the back door lay ajar and Lorcan pushed it open, calling out to announce his arrival. Bridgeen was rolling out flour to make bread and Irinda and Bridgeen's granddaughter Clodagh were mixing a fresh batch in a bowl.

'How's everyone?' beamed Lorcan as he came in.

Irinda carefully put down the wooden spoon she had been using and dusted down her hands on an oversized apron before climbing off her stool and coming over to him.

She motioned to Lorcan to bend closer to her so that she could tell him something.

'My mummy is going to phone later on,' she whispered.

'Oh, how do you know that?' Lorcan asked, bemused by her conspiratorial manner.

'She sent me a text,'

'Oh right,' said Lorcan, for whom such technology was still a mystery.

Suddenly a look of fear came over Irinda's face and she pulled away, pointing over Lorcan's shoulder.

'What's wrong?' he demanded, shocked at the way her face had paled and eyes filled up with tears.

'They're taking my daddy,' said Irinda. 'We have to stop them.'

Lorcan was totally mystified and tried to take Irinda's hand to comfort her, but she pushed past him and ran from the kitchen into an adjoining living room. Bridgeen looked up and Lorcan shrugged as they both followed her into the sitting room. Irinda was standing up close to the widescreen television on which Lorcan could see various heavily armoured men batoning people in a forest. The sound was down and he could not hear what was happening but suddenly the footage cut to a bald, gaunt man dressed in black. Irinda moved forward and reached out to the TV as if trying to touch him.

Lorcan tried to say something to comfort her but could not find the words. From the little girl's reaction he presumed the man was her father and his son. Apart from some photos, in which he had long straggly hair, it was the first time Lorcan had ever seen Irinda's father and he seemed to be standing in the middle of a full-scale riot. Bridgeen was desperately looking for the television remote control as the news channel flashed up a caption.

Lorcan stared in disbelief as the words 'Ecowarrior arrested following fatal shooting' flashed before him.

The pictures showed the man being led by police to a van as the picture of another man was flashed onto the screen with the simple caption: 'Shot dead'.

'Surely to God he didn't do that,' muttered Bridgeen. 'I've seen him on TV before and read about him in the papers and despite that they said he always seemed to be a good man.'

'He is a good man,' said Irinda. 'Why are the police taking him away? What are they going to do with him?'

Finally Bridgeen uncovered the remote control beneath a cushion and she turned up the television volume. Lorcan sat down in an armchair and Irinda climbed up beside him as they watched the news reports from Slovenia and the arrest of the environmental campaigner Wolf Cliss.

'That man is your son and you never told us anything about it,' Bridgeen sighed. 'You're a rare individual Mr O'Malley.'

Lorcan started at the image of the man being dragged away. Irinda's mother had told him that he was involved in environmental campaigns but he'd no idea that Wolf had such a high profile.

'I didn't even know I had a son until about a year ago,' Lorcan said. 'And do you mean to say that you know all about him?'

'Only what I have read in the papers and seen on the TV. He's a famous man Mr O'Malley. I can't believe you have never heard of him.'

Bridgeen, with Irinda throwing in nuggets of incidental detail, began to fill him in on what she knew about Wolf.

PART TWO

10

THROUGH THE NETWORK OF CONTACTS HE had built up in Bonn during his teenage protests against the nuclear cargoes Wolf heard about a punk squat in Amsterdam which was gaining a reputation for militant environmental campaigning. It took Wolf four days to get there, including a night spent in a prison cell for illegally hitching on an autobahn – which actually turned out to be blessing in disguise as it was the only sheltered night's rest and warm meal that he had until he reached the Dutch capital. The squat had been formed by a group of anarchists who had latched onto the punk movement, including a couple of members of a cult punk band called Faecal Loading. The band's drummer, Niels Lunnig, and his French girlfriend, Sophie, had been two of the squat's founding members. Wolf had met Niels when his band had come to play in Bonn at an anti-nuclear festival and the two had impressed one another and so when Wolf arrived at the squat his reputation as an activist had preceded him and a space was cleared on the floor for his sleeping bag. In those days Wolf had short spiky hair and was habitually dressed in torn jeans and black tee-shirts so in terms of image he also fitted in well. While other members of the squat came and went, Wolf, Niels and Sophie remained its core members, surviving evictions, demolitions and numerous personality clashes.

Partly by design, although mostly through fate, Wolf found himself gaining a reputation as an environmental campaigner and labelled with the relatively-new title of ecowarrior. Initially he and his companions in the Dutch squat focused their attention on issues affecting Holland, Belgium, France and Germany – protesting at new road developments, mining operations, industrial pollution and the destruction of forests, fenland and marshes for development. However, as he met protesters from different countries he began to expand his areas of interest and travel further and further afield.

Wolf adopted the style of other ecowarriors and began to grow his hair long and had it plaited into dreadlocks. He was habitually dressed in military-style combat gear but that was as much a practical matter as a fashion statement given that he now spent much of his time living in tents, hastily constructed bivouacs, underground tunnels and tree houses. He was an articulate and passionate speaker with a flair for languages and was thrust to the fore as a spokesman. As well as German he spoke excellent Dutch, English and French, and could converse in a handful of other languages. Although he had dropped out of school aged 18 he was self-educated and could quote everything from international law to the mating habits of obscure Javan insects, just-published scientific research to the lyrics of John Lennon. He became a folk-hero, a multi-lingual ecowarrior who was always at the heart of the action. Quite often, despite himself, he found himself taking physical risks to stop a digger or convoy of lorries passing and this earned him even further kudos among his fellow protesters. He turned up in the Antarctic, New Zealand, England, the Amazon, Norway and India. Upmarket dailies and Sunday supplements lauded him, while downmarket tabloids demonised him as a subversive

He shied away from belonging to any particular group, preferring to choose the campaigns he wanted to become involved in, however, he developed a close relationship with an Argentinean collective called Selva Global. He met some of their members when their ship had docked in Holland during a visit to raise awareness in Europe about the depletion of the ozone layer in the extreme south of Argentina and Chile which had already caused instances of skin cancer among people living there to quadruple. Wolf helped facilitate the visit and set up meetings with sympathetic groups in Europe and worked as a spokesman when they sailed to Britain. At the end of the European visit he travelled on with them and took part a campaign focusing on the destruction of the Amazonian rain forest and the forced uprooting of indigenous communities to make way for mining and engineering projects. It was a major success and Wolf's participation helped raise awareness back in Europe about what was happening. The combination of environmental campaigning and working with indigenous communities whose traditional homes were threatened by big business spread across the Pacific Ocean to Asia and Wolf spent several months on the island of Sumatra during a period of intense logging when huge swathes of rainforest were being cleared. Selva Global hoped that by sending him there he would once again draw the attention of Europeans to what was happening and help put pressure on the financial institutions which were backing the deforestation.

Wolf also spent time trying to engage with communities and

their grassroots political representatives where the logging companies were working. The international corporations preferred to recruit from these communities so that they could justify their activities with the claim that they were bringing employment and economic benefits to the regions that they were destroying. Working with Indonesian activists, Wolf embarked on an educational lecture tour highlighting the irreversible damage to woodland that intense logging caused and the detrimental impact it had had on other communities. The destruction of the Sumatran forests had left large areas of land that had been covered by trees for thousands of years reduced to scrubland that quickly dried out and often caught fire. These fires spread quickly and sometimes ignited neighbouring forests that had survived the logging, only to be incinerated. A huge acrid smog hung over the region, forcing airlines to divert their flights and causing breathing difficulties for those who lived below it.

Wolf suddenly found himself in demand as a commentator and was the subject of a number of television documentaries. He was also commissioned to write articles for newspapers and magazines and by going back to the very human impact of what was happening he found a whole new audience for his environmental message. He used simple language and focused on individual stories to make his point rather that try to contextualise everything into a global saga of corporate destruction.

As his campaigning credentials grew so did his skill at handling the media, however, that created its own problems and he became a victim of his success. Being who he was and doing what he had done had given him a platform to voice his concerns and articulate his philosophy but it also turned him into a media cliché and Wolf found that he and other environmental campaigners had become part of the world of entertainment. What they were saying was entirely valid and he believed that they were genuinely trying to make a difference but he had been turned into a cartoon character by the media making him an easy target for governments and big business to demonise the campaigns he was involved in. Others took it to an even further extreme and tried to undermine him by describing him as an ecoterrorist with the implication that those campaigns he was involved in were subversive and that by supporting them people could undermine the stability of society. Even among fellow environmental campaigners there were detractors and Wolf was often accused of being cynical – someone who was more interested in self-publicity than the issues on whose behalf he was supposed to be campaigning. Wolf understood this, often individuals and groups would work on a single issue for years, protesting, lobbying and working through the courts with little or no recognition then suddenly the dreadlocked German ecowarrior would sweep in like an anti-establishment pop star, pontificate and get dragged about the place in front of the TV cameras and then move on to something else. He justified his freelance attitude by arguing that his high profile at protests brought publicity and attention that they would not generally have received and he always tried to liaise with those working on the ground to ensure that he had their support, however, he was still regarded by the better-known environmental groups as a self-publicist and a maverick. Wolf brazened it out and said nothing, half smiling to himself at the irony, for despite his public persona Wolf squirmed under the attention he received and had to force himself to endure a constant barrage of intensely private crucifixions beneath the macho swagger.

11

LORCAN O'MALLEY HAD GROWN UP IN a rural part of Co Derry where the parish priest ruled his flock like an eastern European dictator. His parents took their religion by rote, attending mass, confession and kneeling on the kitchen floor every evening with their children at 6pm to recite the Angelus. This family adherence to religious duties was reinforced by school until Lorcan was in his mid-teens. He was a tall, gangly youth who towered over his classmates but who was demonised for his constant refusal to fight his more diminutive contemporaries whose fragile machismo was bolstered by baiting someone who would run rather than fight. His timid nature was put down to scholarliness and he was feted at home and school as an intellectual, although Lorcan himself knew that he was not the brilliant student that he was being cast as. Nevertheless it brought advantages and he was given privileges at school such as avoiding sports and being allowed to sit in the library and lose himself in books. This could have brought down greater contempt upon

Lorcan's head, however, a growing reputation as a musician earned him a certain amount of kudos.

Lorcan's grandfather played the fiddle and had started to teach the boy when he was about 10 but when a neighbour handed him a mandolin Lorcan found his true musical calling. The notes on a mandolin and fiddle were the same and Lorcan could follow his grandfather's trembling fingers and pick out the tunes he played until he was able to accompany him. He would travel with his granda to ceilis in neighbouring villages and was regularly called upon to do a turn at weddings, christenings and other family events.

Although he did not do particularly well in his exams, Lorcan's scholarly reputation and a recommendation from Father Moclair, the parish priest, managed to secure him a place at university in Dublin. The priest even arranged digs for him and called to his parents' house to drive him to the bus station on the day he headed off.

In the car the priest confided his hopes for Lorcan's future.

'I was like you too you know. Scorned because I was regarded as an intellectual but it is nothing to be ashamed of. The country needs people like you and the days of farming are numbered. We haven't learned our lessons from the Famine, Ireland can no longer sustain so many people living on the land. We need people with brains to bring businesses to our community. Don't forget us.'

Lorcan nodded solemnly as he got out of the car and hefted his trunk from the roof rack.

'Thanks Father,' he said. However, his mind was haunted by a single thought. He wanted to go to a strip club. He was unsure if any existed in Dublin at that time but the notion had come to obsess him after he read a report about such a venue in a newspaper.

He shuddered at the thought.

Despite attending a few lectures at university, more as a sense of duty to his extended family who had scrapped together the money to send him there than a genuine attempt to become a dedicated student, Lorcan quickly concluded that life in academia was not suited to him. He knew that the mantle of scholar which had been foisted on him was simply a role that he had been playing, for while he was not stupid and had a genuine thirst for knowledge it would have to be from his own self-chosen curriculum. He continued to go to the classes that interested him and spent a lot of time in the university library but the books he chose had little to do with the Anglo Irish literature that he was supposed to be studying. He devoured books about the lives of artists and spent hours pouring over those which carried prints, particularly Van Gough, Gaughan, Klimt and Egon Schiel. He was drawn to artists who seemed to combine debauched lives with high art and shuddered at the penalties they seemed to have paid in terms of health and sanity.

He continued to play mandolin and became involved in the emerging traditional music and folk revival that was happening. For many people in Dublin the music had been regarded as the preserve of culchies, however, the success of Bob Dylan and other folk singers and the endorsement by members of the Rolling Stones and the Beatles had lent it a new credibility. Lorcan who had been immersed in the music since childhood was a welcome arrival to the scene and quickly became a much sought after addition to many of the loose collection of groups who were coming together.

It was with a traditional folk group called Coill, which featured himself on mandolin, a Cork man called Dermot Joyce on flute and Donegal fiddler Eoghan Roarty that he settled, mainly because of Eoghan's tales of touring in Europe. He had gone the previous year and was full of stories of good money to be made, free-loving folkie women and plenty of drink. After just three rehearsals together they had enough common material between them to sustain a couple of hours performance and decided to chance their arm on the continent. They travelled by boat to Wales and by train and bus to Dover where they caught a ferry to France. From there they hitched to Antwerp and played their first gig as the interval act during a strip show. Lorcan had never mentioned his obsession and Eoghan had been almost shy when telling his fellow musicians the sort of venue where he had booked them into. Dermot laughed nervously and Lorcan nodded solemnly as he could, barely able to contain his delight.

The strip club was close to the port in the cellar of a crumbling warehouse. The musicians looked at each other apprehensively as they took to the stage wondering how the hell they were going to keep 200 shit-faced and sex-starved sailors entertained when what they had paid for beer and wobbling naked female flesh.

'We'll pass on the slow airs then,' said Lorcan as he strummed on his fragile mandolin, struggling to hear if it was even in tune amid the shouts and insults emanating from the stink of smoke and sweat just a few feet in front of him.

'Maybe we should just do a strip ourselves … there's bound to be a few of them who like that sort of stuff,' said Dermot.

'I don't think they'd notice any difference to tell you the truth,' said Eoghan. 'You might get more than you bargained for.'

'Would youse just fucken play,' insisted Lorcan.

They were in luck for just as they were about to begin the crew from an Irish cargo ship poured in and screamed with delight as the three musicians launched into O'Neill's March. As they played, their compatriots hurled themselves around the bar in a crazed jig, knocking tables, chairs, drinks and other customers who were too close to the stage flying, causing a mini riot before the other assorted nationalities got into the mood and began to join in.

They were only due to play 15 minutes sets once every hour between the strip routines but as the night went on they ended up backing a couple of the dancers with Lorcan grinning with delight as they swayed just in front of him, turning to jiggle their breasts and gyrate their naked crotches inches from his face like real-life sheela na gigs. Somewhat guiltily he remembered Father Moclair's farewell speech to him but decided that any latent Catholic guilt would have to be suppressed for a while.

When the strip club closed Lorcan and his band mates went to a party with three of the strippers who were smitten by the fast talking Irishmen. They brought their instruments to the apartment the girls shared and between tunes they supped on Belgian beer, smoked joints and charmed their hosts. In the early hours of the morning Lorcan found himself burrowing in what seemed to be slow motion into the fleshy thighs of a girl called Andrea and later contentedly caressing her as she lay sleeping beside him.

They stayed for a week in Antwerp and although Dermot was keen to stay on Lorcan and Eoghan insisted that they use the money that they had made to travel. Much as Lorcan loved the sensual delights of Antwerp he wanted to see as much of the continent as he could. The strip club owner tried to book them for a month but when they said they were determined to go he gave them a list of names and a written reference for club owners in the Netherlands, Denmark, Sweden and Germany and pleaded with them to return to his club for a two-week stint on their return journey.

Using their contacts and those made by Eoghan on his earlier trip they were able to make a comfortable living travelling and playing throughout northern Europe in a series of strip joints, brothels, down-at-heel bars and even an occasional respectable folk club. There was little room for musical finesse as the venues they played were usually hard-drinking joints were the clientele communicated by roaring at one another. Despite this the three musicians developed into a tight-knit unit, their sets given a harder edge and energy by the venues they ended up playing in. They even managed to make an album during a four-week stay in Sweden after falling in with the stars and film crew of a porn movie. A music producer who was making a fortune churning out sleazy muzak soundtracks for Sweden's burgeoning blue movie industry insisted on paying for studio time after he heard them play. What they recorded was basically their live set but when they played it back it sounded lame as the studio gave them no opportunity to reproduce the energy of their stage shows. The producer didn't seem to mind and insisted that he still wanted to put out the record and asked for a few more melodic pieces. Lorcan had composed a couple of tunes on his mandolin, including a piece called 'Mactíre', which he quickly taught to Dermot and Eoghan and which were credited to him on the LP which was only ever released in Sweden and Norway.

12

WOLF HAD MET KEI DURING A protest in northern England against the construction of an industrial estate close to fen land. The developers planned to drain a nearby lake and the fen to prevent water seeping onto their site. However, the protesters had claimed that this would destroy the habitat of more than a hundred different animal, insect and plant species, including rare narrow-leaved marsh orchids. The campaign had been low-key and even the arrival of Wolf and other prominent environmental campaigners failed to ignite much media interest. The protesters were allowed to set up a camp on a farm beside the fen, making it impossible for the developers to evict them and every day they blocked the access the routes to the lake and fen. It was a hot summer and the police were lethargic. Private security guards were called in but after they attacked and hospitalised one of the protesters they were quickly withdrawn as the developers feared a PR fiasco. They wanted to keep the whole thing low key and began to work a series of submissions through the courts to force the police to be more pro-active.

Wolf was enjoying himself, basking in the sun with the other protesters on the tracks that led to fen. He noticed Kei about a week after he arrived when she and a number of other people came to sit close to where they were protesting to eat a picnic. Someone told him that they were archaeologists, employed by the developers to excavate the site where the proposed industrial park was to be built. There was some debate among the environmentalists about whether they should heckle the dig team but Wolf cautioned against it and went over to talk to them. He could see them tensing as he approached but he excused himself and asked if he could join them.

'I suppose you are going to lecture us on why we should abandon the dig and come and join you,' teased Kei.

'Not at all,' said Wolf. 'Maybe you will find a Saxon village or something and the whole thing will have to be put on hold.'

'I doubt it, though that would be nice,' sighed Kei. 'The most interesting thing we have come across so far is a small piece of Chinese pottery."

'Well that's interesting surely, I mean how did it get here? Does that mean there were Chinese traders in this part of England?' asked Wolf, genuinely startled at news of the find.

'Don't think so,' mused Kei.

'Can you really be sure that it comes from China?'

'Well the words 'Made in China' were a bit of a giveaway. A classic period piece … late 1970s we think.'

'Ah,' sighed Wolf.

'There was a piece of Lego as well,' called out one of the other archaeologists. 'Maybe there were trade links here with Legoland.'

Wolf laughed and without thinking took a sandwich from a lunchbox offered to him by Kei.

'Ah,' he sighed again catching sight of a piece of pink flesh wedged in between the pieces of bread.

'What's wrong?' asked Kei.

'Dead pig,' said Wolf nodding towards the ham slice.

'Oh no! You're vegetarian? I'm so sorry that was so silly of me.'

'Don't worry about it.'

The other dig members began tidying up their picnic leftovers and making ready to leave but Kei sat on.

'So how long do you plan to protest here?' she asked Wolf.

'Oh these things have a pattern,' he replied. 'We are still at the phoney-war stage with a token stand-off, but eventually the developers will secure their court orders and we will be forced to move by the police. There will be a couple of days of scuffles, we will all be arrested and the diggers will move in and another little oasis will be subsumed into the concrete jungle.'

'But its not that unique. I know there are rare plants – I have read one of you leaflets – but it is not an endangered species.'

'No, but you let this one go and that is one less, and the numbers are not finite. I doubt the people who hunted the last dodo thought they were about to wipe it out. They just thought there must be more somewhere so it will do not harm to kill this one.'

'Is that not a bit dramatic?' asked Kei.

'That's what I thrive upon.'

'So you are all drama and no substance?'

'I hope not. But lets face it the plight of the narrow-leaved marsh orchid is not one that generates much public excitement or debate. Who cares if it dies out – you can't eat it or make anything with it. It takes the drama of us idiots throwing ourselves in front of diggers and getting dragged off site by our dreadlocks to make people pay attention.'

'And do you get a kick out of that attention?' asked Kei.

Wolf shrugged.

'OK, so maybe the whole thing pampers my inflated ego. But

hopefully as my head swells with the public adulation there will be a couple of narrow-leaved marsh orchids just getting on with existing.'

The dig team were leaving, with one or two waiting impatiently for Kei to follow them.

'There is a pub in the town called The Roebuck in the Thicket. We go there most evenings,' said Kei following her colleagues.

Wolf walked back to his own accomplices.

'Well were you able to get through to them?' asked one.

'Its a work in progress,' replied Wolf smiling to himself. 'Anybody fancy going for a pint tonight?'

When Wolf entered the pub later that evening with a couple of his fellow protesters there were good natured jeers from the group of archaeologists sitting around a table and a space was cleared for them to sit along with them with one woman conspicuously moving from where she sat beside Kei and gesturing for Wolf to take her place.

As Wolf had predicted the developers were given the go-ahead to move the protestors and the diggers moved in. Wolf moved with Kei to her rented London flat and told his colleagues that he was taking a break from campaigning. She was committed to working on a number of digs in England that summer and he travelled with her, staying in hotels, helping out on the digs as an odd job man and labourer and generally not doing very much at all. Kei was passionate about her work and doubted that she and Wolf had that much in common but she was prepared to enjoy the excitement of a fling during her remaining months in England. She had taken little interest in environmental issues and was quick to reprimand Wolf when she felt he was lecturing her about something. It was an eye-opener for Wolf for it made him realise that he could be very annoying and patronising. He was used to living and associating with fellow activists, people who shared his outlook and environmental concerns and who generally agreed with what he said. In fact in recent years his ecowarrior credentials ensured that people rarely disagreed with him and those who did so were simply branded as capitalists who probably supported the very projects which Wolf and his colleagues were protesting against. In a way it was quite humbling to meet someone like Kei who he enjoyed being with and whose life interested him but who refused point blank to defer to any superior wisdom he might imagine that he had. While Kei conceded that there were environmental issues that needed to be addressed she also argued that global industrialisation was necessary for humanity.

'Do you really imagine that we can all go back to living in some utopian idle where we live off the land and build out homes form dead branches and leaves?' she demanded. 'Look at the civilizations where that still happens – the life expectancy is probably 40 and child mortality is rampant.'

'I have never argued for that,' insisted Wolf. 'What I am saying is that the way we live is not sustainable. Of course we need food and water and materials to build a dwelling to suit the climate where we live but human demand has far exceeded that. We are digging out minerals to create machines that can transport you from one place to another as quickly as possible, that feed on liquids whose extraction has a detrimental impact on the environments in which they are found and whose by-products pollute the atmosphere. Other minerals are extracted for pure decoration with the mining process often requiring the use of toxic chemicals that poison the land making it uninhabitable for other species. We are getting to a stage where parts of the Earth are actually becoming uninhabitable and whole species are being killed off due to man-made environmental conditions. Islands have been contaminated by radioactive fallout or swamped by rising oceans, fertile land has been so intensively farmed and forests so effectively cleared to a point that they have become barren desert while the very water that people once drank is being poisoned by toxic discharges.'

'So are you saying that if we don't all do what you are say that the Earth is doomed?' demanded Kei.

'In the long term the Earth will survive. It is much more durable than the creatures who live on it. But we are changing the conditions on the planet that allowed humans to evolve and thrive in the first place. The Earth will survive anything that humans can to do it but whether it will still be in a condition in which humans can live is debatable.'

After a few months living together in England, Kei joined an archaeological dig in Algeria and Wolf, who could see no reason to stay in London by himself, returned to Amsterdam where Niels and Sophie were now actually paying rent to live in an apartment. They had kept a spare room free for Wolf for whenever he was in the city. He kept in touch with Kei by post and the occasional phone call although both seemed to be happy to take a break from what had become an intense and rather fractious relationship.

Wolf agreed to take part in a campaign in southern Spain where a housing development and business park were being built and a nearby river was being diverted to supply them, cutting off natural irrigation to a forest. For Wolf such campaigns were a means of articulating his central philosophy. In a way it was almost too easy to pontificate on the evils of clubbing to death cuddly seal pups – images of their huge vulnerable eyes and blood-splattered white fur were far more effective than any words of outrage ever could be – nuclear arms and power stations were also an emotive issue with stock images and vocabulary that campaigners could draw upon, and the same for rain forests and industrial pollution. The housing development in Spain was not glamorous and of little interest to most people outside the region who were divided anyway between the majority who welcomed the economic benefits and new homes that the project would bring to the area and the few who dared suggest that preserving a few trees and the shelter they provided to mostly non-endangered species was more important. However, for Wolf, like the campaign against the industrial estate in northern England that he had been involved in earlier that year when he met Kei, such issues flagged up the core of the dilemma that was facing mankind. The loss of the small forest in Spain and fenland in England would not have a huge impact on the global environment but they were part of the chipping away process that was going on. A shower of rain on a mountain would not dissolve it overnight but it would wash away a bit of sediment and loosen up a bit of soil and erode a little bit of rock – not enough to be noticeable to the eye but a quantifiable amount that would in turn be washed away in the next shower of rain. It was these minute erosions that over the centuries would eventually change the shape of the mountain and in turn over hundreds of millennia see what once seemed immovable pared down to a stump. Wolf used the analogy to illustrate how the small, micro issues such as an obscure piece of fen land or nameless clump of trees were the symptoms of a global cancer gnawing away at disparate parts of the world but which over time would start to link up and infect the areas that surrounded them before gathering their own momentum and creating huge swathes of wasteland. The Earth's ecosystem was like the mountain – seemingly vast, varied and unchanging, but slowly and almost imperceptibly being eroded until one day nothing would be left.

One of the main activists in the Spanish campaign was Imma Mateus and almost without thinking about what he was doing Wolf began an affair with her. He did not dwell too deeply on what the implications were for his relationship with Kei, although he had to admit to himself he did not want her to find out. It was the first time that he had been faced with such a dilemma for in the past his relationships with women had been brief, transient affairs that involved little emotion, at least on his part. When he was honest with himself he had to admit that he used his celebrity and notoriety to attract women, like a rock star attracted groupies. As far as he was concerned that was fine as long as he did not lead those who became involved with him along and suggest that there was more to his interest in them than the purely physical. However, he felt that his relationship with Kei had been more than a mere transient affair.

On top of that Imma was not the sort of woman who went along for transient relationships either. Her father was a politician for the Spanish conservative party and her maternal grandfather had been a minister in the dictator General Franco's government. She'd had a wealthy and privileged upbringing and was used to getting her own way. She quickly sensed that Wolf had concluded that she was a spoilt rich kid looking for a cause to get involved in to draw attention to herself. To start with that had been true and she relished the discomfort that her activities brought to her bourgeois family and their associates. Many of her father's friends were involved in the businesses whose activities she was campaigning against. However, the more she became involved in campaigning, the more her commitment to the cause of the environment became genuine. She often had to endure mockery from other activists because of her educated Madrid accent and her family's political pedigree but she persisted and when former detractors began to drop away she was still there, earning the respect of those she worked with. She retained a slightly haughty exterior but that was as much a defence against the ragged bonhomie of her fellow campaigners that despite her attempts to join in she could never quite master. Although she was highly regarded by seasoned environmental campaigners, those who met her for the first time tended to make the same judgment that Wolf had – spoilt, rich kid out for some kudos and kicks. The label rankled particularly when it was stuck on to her by someone with the stature of Wolf. She was determined to assert herself, in her own eyes at least, as someone who was an equal with him.

Imma spoke excellent German and when Wolf arrived she immediately set about briefing him on the state of the protest and the various legal options which they were still exploring. Wolf had nodded and questioned her, seeming to accept her expertise on the issue, but then she got the impression that he was looking round for the true leader – who he probably suspected did not speak German and had delegated Imma to fill him in before making him or herself known. Imma was having none of it and began to bark out a few instructions to others involved in the campaign to organise a protest and advise the local and national media that the seasoned German ecowarrior Wolf Cliss was in town and backing their cause. She felt a bit hammy and as if she was showing off but that was they way she operated normally and no-one questioned her authority to do so. It seemed as if Wolf's attitude to her changed and he accepted that she was the campaign leader. He started writing out a few sentences in ungrammatical Spanish and asked her to help translate words and phrases for the press conference that was being organised.

Over the next few days Imma and Wolf were constantly at each other's sides as Spanish newspaper and TV news channels descended on the protest camp to interview the iconic eco warrior.

Wolf was usually able to make a brief statement and then relied on Imma to translate the questions that were fired at him and his replies. As the Spanish campaigners hoped, their profile was raised and the building project was put on hold as planners agreed to reconsider the proposal.

That night the protesters, whose numbers had been boosted following the additional publicity, celebrated with a party at which a number of musicians and street performers appeared. Wolf was happy to join in, although previous experience told him that the planners move was simply a stalling tactic and that they would give the development the go-ahead as soon as Wolf had gone away and all the media attention died down. Imma was ebullient and her slightly distant persona was broken down for the evening. Her association with Wolf had made her into a minor celebrity and she was happy to indulge in limelight, although she too knew at the back of her mind that they had been given a stay of execution rather than an outright victory. The party continued late and despite the constant attention of others there Wolf and Imma kept gravitating towards one another and it seemed to both that it was inevitable that Wolf would end up returning with Imma to her tent. They tried to conduct their affair surreptitiously which was of course naive and when a huge-selling gossip magazine got wind of the fact that the rebellious daughter of a right-wing politician was sleeping with a man who had been dubbed an ecoterrorist it made the front page with both their pictures splashed across it.

Wolf was shocked for while he was used to publicity, both positive and negative, it had never before involved his private life. And it was not just gossip magazines that ran with the story. Spain's normally non-sensationalist newspapers, which had to date focused on the environmental and economic implications of the story, began to take a greater interest in the relationship and soon discovered that one of the businessmen behind the proposed housing development was a close associate of Imma's father. On the back of this the more serious-minded newspapers were able to rather mischievously mention Wolf and Imma's affair.

Wolf suspected that there was a more sinister agenda behind all this salacious gossip for it was causing discomfort among some of their fellow campaigners who felt they were being sidelined by the now-celebrity couple. Things went from bad to worse when a magazine ran with a front cover showing two pictures – one of Wolf with Kei and the other of Wolf with Imma. Wolf didn't need anyone to translate the headline 'Infidelidad'.

Imma was apoplectic, her accusations inarticulate slurs mixing the sibilant syllables of Spanish with the guttural gargles of German.

'We have to turn this round,' Wolf tried to explain to her. 'Why do you think all this scandal is published? It is purely to take away from the core issue that we are campaigning on.'

'Well they wouldn't have any scandal if you had at least been honest and told me that you were in another relationship.'

'I don't think that is an issue any more,' sighed Wolf, for he knew that the magazine also had an English language edition and suspected that Kei, or one of her friends in London, would soon catch wind of what was going on.

Imma agreed to call a press conference and translate for him. Wolf had fully intended opening it by saying that his and Imma's, and Kei's, private lives were matters for themselves and to urge a refocusing on the campaign to save the small forest. However, he quickly realised that he had made a major error of judgment when he arrived for the press conference and saw journalists from British, Dutch and German tabloids among the swollen ranks of the Spanish media. The press conference was a disaster with every attempt by Wolf and Imma to speak about the environmental campaign ignored and shouted down by questions about their sex life and Wolf's infidelity. No-one noticed that while the press conference was taking place the planners reaffirmed planning permission for the housing and business park development. The majority of those who had taken part in the protetst, by now totally disillusioned by the spectacle they had been dragged into, had dispersed by the time Wolf and Imma left the hotel where the press conference had taken place. The couple were followed to the campsite and constantly photographed as they separately took down their tents, which had been pitched beside one another, packed their belongings and walked at a slight distance apart to the train station. The photographers only left them when they disembarked at Madrid where Imma nodded a brief farewell as Wolf waited for a connecting train to Barcelona and onwards to Paris and then Amsterdam. Imma went to stay with friends. Three weeks later pipes were laid to divert the river to the site of the proposed development. The trees in the forest didn't get a chance to die from thirst as they were chopped down and their wood used to build garden fences, some of them in the new housing development.

Wolf had often been accused of being a paranoid conspiracy theorist but following his experiences in Spain he did feel somewhat justified in concluding that someone was out to get him.

13

DERMOT, EOGHAN AND LORCAN EVENTUALLY arrived in West Berlin where they had been booked to play by a serious folk club. However, the studied listening poses of their audience and the polite clapping unnerved Lorcan after the raucous gigs that he had become used to and when they had finished playing he left by himself, drawn instinctively to the seedier streets where the strip clubs and brothels lay. Despite having spent nearly every night of the last six months playing in such places, Lorcan was apprehensive, for he was going this time as a voyeur rather than as a performer. He paid his way in to the first club that caught his eye and found a seat in a shaded alcove close to the bar where he watched the half-hearted performance on stage. The club was nearly empty with just a handful of punters sitting in isolated pools of darkness. However, in a corner three women sat smoking and chatting easily to one another. Despite the girl who was slowly divesting her clothes on the spot-lit stage, Lorcan's eyes kept darting towards them. They were all wearing coats, but one had let hers slip enough from her shoulders for Lorcan to see the glitzy garb of a stripper beneath.

He knew there was no point approaching as he would be dragged swiftly away by one of the bouncers and told not to bother the girls. He had seen it happen enough times before and relished being in the privileged position of being a fellow performer with every right to go and chat to the strip artists. The girls he had met during his tour of Europe were so used to being pawed and groped in the clubs were they worked that they tended to only socialise with other workers in the club – barmen, bouncers and band members, and sometimes, though not always, sleep with them. In the months that he had been on the road Lorcan had had a raft of flings and one night stands with girls who worked in the clubs.

He was thinking of this when he noticed one of the girls had got up and was walking towards him. He tried not to look at her too eagerly, aware that she probably got a dozen hang-dog glances pleading for attention every time she tossed her hair and so was shocked when she came and sat beside him.

'I saw you and your friends playing in Munich last week,' she said. 'You're Irish, right?'

Lorcan nodded, trying to recall the girl but he couldn't.

'I don't remember seeing you there?' he said.

'No? I wasn't dancing that night. I just called in to see some friends before I left to come back here. I couldn't believe it. I have never seen the club so lively. I was almost tempted to stay.'

'I wish you had,' said Lorcan shyly.

The girl introduced herself as Mandy and at the end of the night after he had watched her and her companions dance Lorcan went with her to her apartment. They spent all the next day in bed and, although Lorcan was due to meet Eoghan and Dermot that evening, when he found out that Mandy was not working he did not want to leave her, or her apartment. When he poked his head out through a window he could see the Berlin Wall at the end of the street and on the other side the communist-controlled part of the city. He got a strange thrill from making love to Mandy in her creaking iron bed in her ancient flat within metres of the impenetrable border between east and west.

The next day Lorcan managed to drag himself away and tracked down his two band mates in a bar close to the hotel where they were staying. He immediately sensed a change in mood since the last time he had seen them.

'What's up?' he asked.

'This eejit is missing his ma and wants to go home,' sighed Eoghan, nodding at Dermot.

'Its not that but how long are we going to go on like this playing strip joints and ropey folk clubs and staying in mangy hotels?' replied Dermot. 'We had a good time and I'm just saying maybe its time to start heading back.'

Lorcan was alarmed. He couldn't imagine going back to Ireland, especially when he had just met Mandy, who was due see again in the club where she worked later that evening.

'Would you not consider staying for another while? I mean Berlin seems like a good spot and we were taken seriously by that folk club crowd. We could maybe refine our material,' he said.

Eoghan smiled.

'Where have you been for the last 36 hours anyway?' he demanded.

'I don't like to brag,' replied Lorcan. 'What do you think Dermy?'

However, the flute player was not to be persuaded and seemed to have his heart set on leaving as soon as possible.

'We have an album under our belts now, maybe we could go back and actually do this seriously. We're a good tight group,' he said.

Eoghan nodded slowly.

'Well it might be worth a try – remember the Beatles and their return from Hamburg?' he said.

'I'm staying for a while,' insisted Lorcan. 'Maybe I'll come home for Christmas, but I want to stay here for a bit.'

The other two looked startled but did nothing to try and dissuade him. When Lorcan met Mandy that night and told her that his band mates were returning to Ireland while he stayed on she immediately offered to let him stay in her apartment.

'At least until you find somewhere for yourself,' she added hastily.

Mandy helped Lorcan find work in a small second-hand book shop where the shelves were crammed tightly with mostly German volumes, but also with a sizeable collection of English and French titles. The winter that Lorcan lived in Berlin was a bitter one, with thick snow packed tightly onto the streets. The shop was heated by a small gas fire whose spluttering flame bathed it in a flickering orange glow, which along with the musty smell of the books were Lorcan's abiding memory of the place. There were few customers and Lorcan was left mostly in peace to gaze indolently into the dancing tongue of flame or browse through some volume chosen at random. He made a bit of extra money by playing mandolin two or three nights a week in various bars and even took a few classes to teach aspiring musicians a few Irish tunes.

In the summer Lorcan and Mandy caught a bus with a bunch of hippies along the autobahn through East Germany and into the west, across into France, down through Spain and over to Morocco. They stayed in a cheap hotel in Essaouira where Lorcan was dismayed to learn he had just missed seeing Jimi Hendrix who had been in the town a few weeks earlier. When in Berlin, Lorcan had smoked an occasional joint but the hash in Morocco was in a different league and Lorcan was almost permanently stoned for the two months that they stayed there.

While Mandy was not adverse to the odd spliff she told Lorcan that she was wary of drugs and urged him to cut down his intake. Despite her pleas Lorcan continued to smoke constantly, unable to even get out of bed without first smoking a joint and regularly topping himself up throughout the day. Mandy caught the bus to nearby Marrakech and went camping for a few days with a group of Germans into the Atlas mountains but Lorcan spent all his time stoned in their hotel room, occasionally dragging himself to lie on the beach or to sit in a cafe and giggle with other bombed-out hippies. It was only when Mandy told him that she was leaving and returning to Berlin that he forced himself to come down from his extended trip and face up to the practicalities of having to either go with her or be stranded in Essaouira without her and before long without any money.

Back in West Berlin, Lorcan and Mandy found themselves exactly where they had been before they left with Mandy returning to work five nights a week in the strip club and Lorcan to the second-hand bookshop and occasional pub gig.

Lorcan had enough German to get by in most day-to-day situations, including dealing with customers in the shop, but it was limited. His poor German, along with his long hair and beard, made the chances of getting a well-paid job in Berlin unlikely. Mandy hated having to work as a stripper although it was fairly well paid, and the money that Lorcan earned was pitiful in comparison. But when she suggested that they go to Ireland, or even England, where he would have a better chance of getting work Lorcan shuddered at the thought and dismissed such an option. His relationship with Mandy was often intense with bitter rows followed by passionate reconciliation. Sometimes the tension between them was unbearable and he wondered why they should both put themselves through such a situation. He sometimes felt a vague yearning to move on again but could not imagine doing so without Mandy and the thrill of living in the centre of Europe had not worn off, particularly so close to one of the major interfaces of the Cold War which was then at its height.

From the fourth-floor apartment where Lorcan lived with Mandy he often gazed from the window at the concrete slabs topped with barbed wire blocking off the end of the street. Beyond it and over a stretch of wasteland he could see another street with people walking and cars parked outside their homes – other lives lived, and he presumed at least some of them as intensely as his. One night, when Mandy had gone off to work in the strip club Lorcan sat staring out from their apartment window towards the wall and he promised himself that the next day he would try to muddle his way through the bureaucratic process necessary to obtain a visa to visit the east of the city. He wanted to stand in the street on the other side of the wall and look back over to where he lived. He was impatient and began to pace around the apartment, eager to be doing something but disinclined to go out to the bar where he played and his usual cronies hung out. He picked up an ornamental box he had bought in Morocco the previous summer and where he kept his stash of dope and cigarette papers. Although he had cut back his intake from the time he had spend in Morocco he still smoked every day, although he tried to restrict himself to smoking in the evenings. He was about to roll himself a joint when he noticed a small cellophane package that he had forgotten about among the various bits and pieces. He had bought the LSD from a doorman at the strip club and intended to take it one night when he and Mandy where at home so that she could talk him down if need be. But now he was eager for new experiences and with impatient dexterity pulled the wrapping from the LSD-soaked paper and let it dissolve on his tongue. Lorcan made himself coffee and sat back in his armchair, gazing out the window towards the wall and tried to define the moment when his mind moved from contemplative sobriety into chemical enhanced perception. Just as he thought he had paid for a dud he notice that the walls of the room were starting to undulate, barely perceptibly at first but then more and more pronounced until he was sure he could see them warping towards him before twisting away again – then it was not just the walls but also furniture and carpet, even Lorcan's legs which were stretched out before him that seemed to pulsate.

He found a grain of salt nestling in the fabric of his armchair and nervously began to roll it between his finger and thumb. He could define its contours, dips and rises – it was as if he had a tiny planet in his hand, complete with mountains and valleys strewn over continents and separated by expanses of dried-out ocean. He imagined the earth reduced to such a size and yet still able to contain all life upon it. In the vastness of the universe the earth was just such a speck and perhaps even the universe itself was the size of a grain of salt in a different dimension. Perhaps the universe was like a single cell in a human body, made up of billions of galaxies that in turn contained billions of planets some of which were home to intelligent life in which beings like himself were contemplating the exact same scenarios as he was now – telescoping each component of their body into infinity only to be repeated in an even more impossibly smaller scale until it came full circle – all that existed contained within itself. The vastness of the idea appalled him, but he could not let it go. The tinyness of the grain of salt horrified him but as he rolled it he could feel it begin to expand until it was the size of a football and then into an earth-sized planet, yet still rolling between his finger and thumb. When he looked at it was still the same tiny grain but it rested planet-sized among the contours of his thumbprint. Something in his psyche ruptured as it struggled and failed to contain the idea and he felt himself collapsing onto the floor and rolling himself into a ball as he tried to protect himself from the vastness of the universe. He tried talking to himself and to set mathematical problems to distract his mind, at least for as long as the effects of the LSD continued, but he kept coming back to it. It felt as if the idea had shredded his mind and that he could no longer see a rational pattern in the world in which he lived. Every time he closed his eyes he could see explosions of light streaking between galaxies, pillars of fire across millennia.

14

IT WAS SOPHIE WHO FIRST DESCRIBED them as a bunch of ecopunks. They had never formed an organisation as such, each preferring to campaign on the issues that interested them most but they kept one another up to date with what they were doing and provided back-up and support when needed. However, the term ecopunks came to be associated with the Amsterdam-based activists. One of their associates from the heady days of the commune was Gustav Linser who had returned to his native Austria and studied law and eventually acted on behalf of them in courts throughout Europe. Niels had begun to toy around with computers and technology and soon became a competent computer hacker. When the internet began to grow in popularity he set up websites to help activists communicate and share information with one another although it would be another ten years before they finally hit on the concept of the ecopunks website.

There were others who brought their own skills and areas of expertise to the group. Sophie, trained in alternative medicines and became an accomplished vegan chef. She was also an expert in sustainable living and studied building techniques that utilized natural products and green energy. She spent a year living on a sparsely populated Danish island, starting from scratch to build her own accommodation and a wind-powered generator, foraging for food and eventually farming her own crops. She then made a respectable living giving lectures about her experience and as well as becoming a much sought after environmental speaker Sophie found herself a feminist icon.

When Wolf returned to Amsterdam from Spain he was mocked pitilessly by Sophie and Niels and the other activists who worked with them. He felt emotionally battered following the public exposition of his private life but they had little sympathy for him. At first he resented their attitude but after a while realised that he had perhaps been taking himself too seriously and had to admit that to a large extent the situation was a result of his own actions. While the campaign to save the small forest in Spain had floundered following the salacious expose of Wolf and Imma's affair, Wolf's own standing was ironically enhanced as the media coverage had made him even more widely known than before. His presence was more sought after by campaigners who knew that their causes would be given a major PR boost by Wolf's arrival on the scene. He resented this in many ways and felt that his credentials as a serious environmental campaigner were being undermined by the shallow cult of celebrity that now surrounded him. Others felt the same, both fellow environmentalists and those who he opposed. However, despite his reservations, Wolf swallowed his pride and played up to his celebrity status – only Niels and Sophie knew how he really felt but they encouraged him to milk his profile while it lasted because like most other minor celebrities he would one day be forgotten and irrelevant.

Wolf ran in to Kei again during a campaign in Ireland. He had been asked by a group of activists to join them in a protest against a new road which was being built through bogland which was due to be drained to make way for the construction. He had never told anyone about the Irish father he had never met, not even Niels and Sophie, and felt apprehensive as he travelled through England and Wales by train to catch the ferry to Dublin. However, his concerns were quickly sidetracked when on the sailing across the Irish Sea he noticed two of the archaeologists who had been working with Kei when he first met her the previous year at the dig in England. They spotted him and given their nervous glances into a lounge area Wolf quickly concluded that Kei was with them. Sighing, he went in to the lounge and saw his former lover sitting with her feet up on a table reading a book. As he approached she looked up and frowned, however, before he reached her two teenagers intercepted him and asked him for his autograph. It was one of the aspects of his new-found celebrity that irritated him most and that he found hardest to get used to. He initially thought it was a good way to 'preach' and spread his message but most of those who approached him were really not that interested. Quite a few didn't even know what he was famous for they had just recognized his face and dreadlocks from the television or newspapers and had asked for his autograph. Some thought he was a pop star and others an actor from a soap opera. He obliged the two autograph hunters and fobbed them off before sitting down beside Kei.

'You've become very famous,' she said.

'It's not something I particularly enjoy,' replied Wolf.

Kei raised an eyebrow.

'All those easy lays. Surely you must enjoy it a little bit?'

'Ah,' said Wolf, preparing himself for a confrontation.

'Don't worry,' said Kei. 'You're a free agent and so am I?'

'Oh. Right. So you've met someone else then?' said Wolf, surprising himself at how let-down he felt.

'I did but it's over. So where are you heading?'

Wolf told her about the campaign he had been asked to take part in. Kei nodded thoughtfully.

'It sounds awfully close to the dig we are going to take part in,' she said. 'A couple of bodies have been found in the bog, possibly ritually sacrificed – dating to around 300 BC – and almost perfectly preserved.'

'But how can you excavate a bog?' asked Wolf.

'Traces of a settlement have been found nearby so we are going to dig and try to make a link.'

'It'll still not stop the road being built.'

Kei shook her head.

'We've got three weeks. Another rush job. We seem to spend our time being parachuted in to digs and told to log as much as possible before they are built over.'

'You should start a protest,' said Wolf.

'It'll never catch on,' sighed Kei. 'So are you not going to offer to buy me a drink?'

When they parted at the ferry terminal to make their separate ways to where the proposed road was due to be built it was with a mutual understanding that that they would meet up as soon as they both had settled into their respective roles. Wolf was met by some of the campaigners who drove him in a rattling camper van from Dublin to the Irish midlands where a protest camp had been established. Wolf was businesslike and tried to avoid meeting the eyes of one of the protest leaders who had begun to move in on him almost as soon as they'd met. He was determined not to be distracted by another causal fling although he had a gnawing doubt in his stomach about becoming involved with Kei again. He suspected that a relationship with her would be an all-or-nothing situation where he would have to abandon various aspects of his peripatetic life if he wanted to stay with her. The protest was still at what Wolf referred to as the phoney-war stage where diggers and other equipment had moved in, not to start work but to stake out their territory. The protesters had set up camp in a field with permission of the farmer who owned it and who objected to the road being built. As hoped for by the campaigners Wolf's arrival on the scene engendered a flurry of media interest in the protest and a clutch of reporters, photographers and television crews arrived to interview him. The discovery of the preserved bodies in the bog had generated some useful publicity for the protest and given them a good platform from which to voice their objections. The campaign leaders were well seasoned and Wolf had met one or two of them before so they agreed that he should take a back seat and let them conduct the interviews with Wolf nodding in agreement and throwing in an occasional word of support while providing lots of photo opportunities.

He stood beside the area where the bodies had been found, lay down in front of a digger, which wasn't actually going anywhere, held a placard and addressed a group of protesters through a megaphone.

On the first night he was able to he arranged to meet Kei in a quiet pub.

'I'm turning into a fucking puppet he said,' explaining to her what he had been up to. 'The news agenda has become a series of clichés and I am up there along with the greedy business men and the corrupt politician – a stock image that can be churned out to create a news story that runs to hundreds of words without actually telling you anything about what is happening.'

Kei nodded sympathetically.

'Our dig is going nowhere,' she said. 'The site is a dud so I think we will be finishing up earlier than we thought. Will that mean they will start drainage work?'

'Not for a few weeks. The minister responsible for it has vowed to look at the application again but it is simply a delay until attention dies down.'

'Maybe you should take a holiday and come back when the actual work is due to start. No point hanging around if nothing is happening.'

'What would you suggest?' asked Wolf.

'Cycling. I can hire the bikes if you can provide the tent.'

'I never travel without one,' smiled Wolf.

The following day Wolf told his fellow protesters that he had to meet some other contacts in Ireland but would be back within ten days. He met up with Kei and they caught a bus to the west coast of Ireland before starting their cycling holiday. They had not spoken about how they saw the week developing but Kei assumed that Wolf must have known that it would rekindle their relationship and on the first night there was no question that they would zip their sleeping bags together and become lovers as if the gap of the previous year had not happened. They did not speak about what had occurred between Wolf and Imma, nor did Kei discuss the brief relationship she'd had with a Peruvian geologist called Marco who she had met while working in Egypt and who she had to admit probably still believed that they were merely spending time apart. Kei had thought they would simply just cycle and see where they ended up but Wolf seemed to have a fairly clear idea of they route he wanted them to take through the rugged countryside. After a couple of days he insisted that they take a narrow road that seemed to cut through a barren mountain valley and, as far as Kei's sense of direction could tell, doubled back on the way they had just come.

'Have you been here before?' she asked when they stopped to take a break.

'No, never. Just wanted to get off the beaten track a bit and see the real wilds.'

By early afternoon Wolf stopped again and suggested that they stop for the night and pitch their tent on a bit of rough ground by the side of the road.

'But there is nothing here, hardly even a bush to go behind for a pee,' complained Kei.

'There's a house. Maybe you could go there and ask to use their toilet,' replied Wolf who had already started to unpack his tent. 'I just have a good feeling about this place and want to spend the night here. From tomorrow you can call the shots.'

Kei looked at him quizzically, convinced that he was working to some private agenda but unable to even guess at what that might be. She decided not to argue and began to unstrap her own luggage from the bike and went to a stream to get water for drinking and cooking. When Wolf had erected the tent they sat drinking tea and Kei had to admit that there was a pagan charm about this remote bog surrounded by mountains.

'I wonder who lives there?' she mused nodding towards the house. 'Whoever it is must go weeks without seeing anyone.'

'Maybe that is what he wants?' said Wolf following her gaze. 'Lets call over and ask for directions?'

'I didn't realise we were lost,' sighed Kei getting up to follow Wolf. 'And how do you know it is a he ... could be a family or a woman.'

Wolf seemed to hesitate as he approached the house but pushed open the gate set in a stone wall and walked up the short path where he rapped his knuckles on the wooden door. Kei didn't really expect anyone to answer and was surprised when she heard a rattling bolt being shaken and then pulled back. A tall man with an explosion of curly hair cascading to his shoulders stood before them. That would have been his most remarkable feature if it hadn't been for his eyes, which seemed to gaze at some point beyond where Kei and Wolf were standing, even though he was talking to them. His voice was uncertain but not unfriendly.

'Sorry to disturb you,' said Wolf, looking intently at the man who stood before them. 'We are camped just across the road. I hope you don't mind?'

'No not at all. Its not my land. Do as you please. Do you need anything?' asked the man.

'No just wanted to check it was OK to camp here and ask what is the best way to get to Galway,' said Wolf.

The man smiled and pointed back along in the direction they had come that day, explaining how they could follow a number of routes depending on how much scenery they wanted to see.

'That's great thank you,' said Wolf turning to go.

'No problem,' replied the man. 'Are you German by any chance? Your English is very good but you do have a German accent.'

'No not German. I'm Dutch. Thanks again for you help,' said Wolf gesturing for Kei to follow him.

'Dutch, Right. Vaarwel … have a good trip,' said the man turning and closing the door behind him.

'Why did you lie and say you were not German?' demanded Kei when they had crossed the road again to where their tent was.

Wolf shrugged and looked back towards the house.

'I don't like people asking my nationality. What's it got to do with him anyway?'

'You're the one who went to his house and disturbed him. I

doubt he gets many callers out here. Surely he is entitled to a little bit of curiosity?'

Wolf shrugged again and changed the topic of conversation. They were up early the next morning and back on their bikes and just as they were setting off the man came out of his house and waved over at them. Kei waved back but Wolf ignored him and cycled on.

At the end of the holiday Wolf returned to the protest and Kei to England where Wolf agreed he would meet her when he had finished. It was eight weeks before Wolf arrived and by that time Kei knew that she was pregnant. Wolf took the news in his stride but then began to panic.

'I've never worked in my life. How am I going to support you?'

Kei rolled her eyes.

'Well obviously I didn't snare you for your money,' she sighed. 'I can earn enough to keep us but you will have to help bring up the baby.'

'Fine,' smiled Wolf.

Kei travelled with him to Amsterdam where they found an apartment, close to where Niels and Sophie lived and who were also expecting their first child. Sophie took Kei under her wing to help her work through Dutch bureaucracy, however, they quickly ran in to problems. Kei had a work visa but that did not entitle her to health care.

'You are going to have to get hitched, Wolf,' Sophie said. 'Either that or go and live in Japan.'

The prospect of living in Japan was more appealing to Wolf than getting married and he even suggested it but Kei was not keen to return her homeland and traditional family with the disreputable looking ecowarrior and tell them that she was about to have his child. Wolf was not unhappy at the prospect of becoming a father and had convinced himself that he was content to live with Kei in a monogamous relationship to bring up the child but he had a nagging doubt about getting married.

'It just seems such a conventional thing to do?' he confided to Niels.

'Well its a means to an end. Just a bit of paperwork,' replied Niels.

'I keep telling myself that.'

'Maybe you have doubts about committing to Kei?'

Wolf sighed.

'Yeah maybe that too,' he said.

In the event he and Kei were married at a civil ceremony with Niels and Sophie acting as witnesses. Following their wedding Kei was able to claim German citizenship and get an EU passport. She had secured an advance to write a book on the alternative history theories, which had begun to catch on in the west, for a Japanese audience. She was for the most part rehashing theories which had already been published in numerous books in Europe and north America but with an Asian slant. She was not totally convinced about them but for the sake of the book made a convincing argument.

Wolf contented himself with campaigning in Europe and was never away from Amsterdam for more than a few weeks until their daughter Irinda was born. They continued to live a fairly settled life for another eighteen months until Wolf was asked to take part in a protest in the Pacific Ocean against planned nuclear tests. He though Kei would object, and he almost hoped she would because it was risky venture, however, she agreed as long as he undertook to come and visit her and her family in Japan afterwards.

15

ALTHOUGH HE HAD COME CLOSE TO death on a number of occasions Wolf rarely allowed himself to contemplate it, however, the two weeks he spend drifting at sea in the middle of a nuclear testing zone left him with little option. The French government planned to explode a nuclear device over an isolated area of the Pacific Ocean and all shipping had been diverted from the zone, its perimeter was heavily patrolled by the French navy, with some tacit but unspoken support from its military allies. Never-the-less a number of vessels managed to slip through, including a small yacht called El Acorde Perdido owned by a Californian business woman called Cathy Ovenbeck. As well as Cathy and Wolf the crew consisted of a Jamaican music producer called Francis and a Jordanian environmental activist called Ibrn. At lest 10 other boats planned to break through the cordon, each of them crewed with people from Africa, the Americas, Asia, Australasia and Europe to ensure as much global coverage as possible. There had been no contact with the various vessels before they sailed into the testing zone with each agreeing to keep their strategies and eventual destinations secret from one another to ensure they were not compromised.

The initial exhilaration at managing to sneak past the French cordon and into the exclusion zone was quickly replaced by a stark realisation of the horrendous implications for those who were on board. The French government had made it quite clear that it intended to proceed with its nuclear test regardless of any protesters who entered the area. While it was easy to convince themselves that this was pure bluff the activists now had to consider the harsh reality that the French, backed by their military allies, might carry out their test. Ovenbeck and her crew sailed to a random coordinate, well into the exclusion zone but far enough off centre so as not to be obvious, and simply let the boat drift. All radio communication was banned and the four-man crew found themselves cooped-up on the tiny vessel with stale water and limited rations in sweltering heat, contemplating their probable extinction.

For the first couple of days they could hear and occasionally see aircraft in the distance which they presumed were searching for them and any other vessels which had made it through. There were four French activists scattered among the various crews to maximise opposition in their homeland but Wolf and his companions had no way of knowing if they had made it through. For all they knew they might be the only boat in the exclusion zone.

On the third day they could not see nor hear any aerial activity and Wolf concluded that that the French government had abandoned any further searches and were now preparing to go ahead with the nuclear test, regardless of the presence of any protesters. They could simply argue that those who had sailed into the exclusion zone had done so of their own volition, in the full knowledge that the nuclear device was going to be exploded there.

Kei had told Wolf of the devastation that her grandmother had witnessed in Nagasaki following the detonation of an atomic bomb by the US military in 1945 to force a surrender by Japan. She had seen people still walking as their skin peeled from them and on the pavement the outlines of human forms, people who had simply been vaporised into a film of dust, flash-burnt onto the ground, shadows of what had once been sentient beings blitzed into oblivion without even a millisecond to come to terms with their imminent demise.

Wolf had half hoped that they would be apprehended before breaking through the cordon or else spotted and dragged away by the French military. Although he did not voice any such hope he suspected that the others had felt the same. It was possible that the French were playing a psychological game with them and would give them time to crack and flee before detonating their device. It was down to a game of chicken. Would they sail from the test zone after a token few days there in the full knowledge that they had done their best and that their noble protest had failed, that it was better to live and fight for another day? Once again Wolf half-hoped that someone else would say it, for he was sure they were all thinking it, but everyone remained steadfast.

Wolf wondered if, when the explosion came, he would have time to gather himself together and prepare for his own destruction. Would he see a flash in the sky as the bomb exploded, hear the boom and then wait for the force of the blast to shred the fibres of his body into a billion pieces and disperse them across the bubbling stretches of ocean whose surface had been vaporised at the same instant as Wolf and his companions, the boat and even the surrounding atmosphere? As Wolf stared at the sky he was afraid to even blink in case he should miss his own death. Once out of the corner of his eye he caught sight of a sudden flash and he dared

106

hardly breath as he waited to hear the crash of a nuclear explosion. It took him several seconds to realise that a flash of sun had simply caught in the silver frame of someone's sunglasses. Even if they managed to survive the force of the blast they would quickly be bombarded by radioactive fallout that would either burn their flesh from them or else initiate a slightly slower, but never-the-less inevitable process of decay.

Despite the possibility that the four of them would die together there was no camaraderie between the crew members, no black banter as there had been on other missions. But while some of those had entailed an element of risk, none had been as deadly as this one. Each of them sat in silence and tried to come to terms with the decision they had made. Ovenbeck was a practising Buddhist and spent a lot of time meditating, while Ibrn used his prayer mat to communicate with Allah. Francis had proclaimed himself to be a Rastafarian but did not seem to openly pray or undertake any communication with his god. Wolf had not been brought up in any particular faith and if asked would have declared himself an atheist but when death seemed so inevitable and so imminent he could not help considering if there was an alternative to oblivion. Was it not possible that some elemental spark that existed within his psyche and gave him the ability to perceive himself as an individual would continue to exist after the death of his body?

They kept their radio tuned into an agreed frequency waiting for some communication from the outside world that would seal their fate. After 13 days it crackled in to life with the news that the French had abandoned their plan for the nuclear test following the intervention of a number of governments on behalf of their citizens who were believed to be in the testing zone, including, Wolf was surprised to find out, the German government. He had never felt so scared before and now that it he had been given a reprieve from what had felt like a death sentence he was impatient to be back on land and come to terms with what he had just gone through. However, they were told that one of the other vessels which had been taking part in the protest was in difficulty after being damaged by a large piece of flotsam and took a detour to pick up the crew. They were apprehensive because they wanted to get out of the area as quick as possible in case, now that they had broken radio silence and revealed their coordinates, they were picked up by the French navy or one of their allies. Wolf was due to land with Ovenbeck and the rest of her crew on an island in Micronesia from where he hoped to hitch a lift with one of the Japanese vessels that had been taking part in the protest to meet up with Kei and their daughter.

When they came alongside the damaged vessel Wolf was astounded to see that among its crew was Imma Mateus. He had not seen her since they had frostily parted company at the Madrid train station three years earlier, although he had read in various newspapers and bulletins that she had continued to be involved in environmental and wildlife causes. She had even visited Amsterdam, when Wolf was not there, and made contact with the other ecopunks activists, including Sophie and Niels.

In the general melee of euphoria and relief there was little time for them to rekindle their animosity and they joined in the general hugging and backslapping. The damaged vessel was beyond repair and its crew transported their luggage and remaining supplies onto Ovenbeck's yacht before scuttling theirs. Everyone made space as best they could on the small boat to accommodate the new passengers in the three or four days it would take them to make landfall. That night they celebrated with wine and beer which Ovenbeck had hidden on board in the very hope of being able to have such a celebration. Wolf and Imma skirted about one another, making only small talk and avoiding any mention of their previous encounter. When the drink had run out and they were preparing to retire to bed Wolf offered to give up his berth and sleep on the deck and Ibrn did the same, however, Wolf was woken by a hissed whisper in his ear and was startled to see Imma kneeling beside him.

'Your friend Francis and our captain Serge have hit if off and are fucking like mad in there,' she giggled.

'Surely you're not offended,' said Wolf.

'Not in the least but when we were waiting for that bomb to go off I kept thinking that if I ever lived I would grab the first man that I saw and have him. So far the only men that I have seen have been gay, devout Muslims and you.'

Wolf zipped down his sleeping bag and made space for her to slip in beside him and hoped that Ibrn who was sleeping across the deck from them would not be woken. He thought guiltily of Kei and Irinda but then he reasoned that Kei had never been faced with what had appeared to be the certainty of death and would not be able to understand the pure animal joy of reasserting his basic humanity by experiencing the physically sensual. However, deep down he knew that such a rationalisation would not stand up under later, more considered scrutiny and even as he and Imma began their first tentative exploratory caresses he was contemplating the deception he would have to undertake this renewed infidelity.

When Wolf arrived in Japan, Kei didn't even give him a chance to deliver a cover story. The anti-nuclear protesters had been given wide coverage in the Japanese media as one of the boats in the proposed testing zone had been carrying a Japanese peace activist. While the stories had tended to focus on the country's diplomatic efforts to have the test called off and the native protestor the reports had also contained profiles of others believed to be in the test zone. Kei had been looking out for Wolf's name and had been preparing to show it proudly to her family whose shock at her surprise marriage had been only slightly tempered by delight with their new-born grandchild. However, before Kei came across a profile of Wolf she saw one about Imma and even though she knew they were not necessarily on the same boat she knew that it was possible that they would meet up at some point. From then on, despite her genuine concerns about Wolf, she had a gnawing sense of dread that he would resume his affair with Imma. When the French announced that they had abandoned the proposed nuclear test Kei found herself drawn away from the hard-news reports to western tabloids and gossip magazines. She didn't have to wait long and soon saw a speculative piece in a Spanish magazine reporting that the rebel daughter of the conservative Spanish politician was consorting once again with the notorious 'ecoterrorist' Wolf Cliss. Within days other newspapers and magazines were carrying pictures of the couple cavorting at a celebration on a Pacific island were the various activists had regrouped after their sojourn at sea. At the same time Kei received a phone call from Marco, the Peruvian engineer she'd had a fling with in Algeria three years earlier. He had written her a string of letters declaring his love for her after she had told him that she was back with Wolf that hadn't even relented when she told him that she was pregnant. She was standing in the hallway of her parent's house and could hear Irinda playing with her mother in the next room as she spoke to Marco. She had not told her parents about what she was reading about the son-in-law they had never met. She bit her lip as she heard Marco saying that he was sorry he had pestered her before but he knew what was happening between Wolf and Imma and he simply wanted to offer Kei support. She sighed as she hung up the phone and wondered at how the imagined pre-destined life that she had outlined for herself, Wolf and Irinda could so suddenly be relegated to a half-remembered silly whim. She picked up the phone again and booked a hotel close to the city's airport for the following night and made arrangements for her parents to look after Irinda while she went off on, to them, unspecified business.

By the time Wolf arrived in Japan, Marco had secured a temporary transfer to the Japanese branch of the company he worked for, rented a house for six months and moved in to it with Kei and Irinda.

'The deal is simple,' said Kei when she and Wolf met. 'I will bring up Irinda here in Japan, although we may move to New York next year when Marco has to return to his company's headquarters. I will make sure that Irinda is raised knowing that you are her father and you can come and see her when ever you want, within reason of course. I will bring her to Amsterdam twice a year to see you on dates that suit us both, the rest of the time you will just have to make arrangements to come and see us wherever we are living. I expect you, when you get back to Holland, to ensure that we are divorced as soon as possible. None of this is negotiable.'

Wolf nodded, dumbly shell-shocked by Kei's verbal barrage but could not help looking at Marco who was sitting beside her and wondering how his now ex-wife had managed to find herself in a new stable relationship so quickly while his intense physical affair with Imma had once again descended into bickering and acrimony.

16

LORCAN WAS NEVER REALLY SURE HOW he made it back to Ireland. The days following the fatal LSD trip were more memorable for the terrors that haunted his mind than what was happening in the outside world. He had a vague recollection of Mandy trying to talk to him and others came within and left his field of vision but he could not concentrate on what they were saying to him. At some stage he found himself travelling with Eoghan by coach through East and West Germany and into France from where he was taken by plane from Paris to Dublin and back to his family in County Derry. He hadn't seen them since he had dropped out of university and had only sent them occasional postcards during his year in Europe and north Africa to let them know that he was in good health. He had never sent them a return address and so he'd had no communication from them.

They had been a close family and were shocked by Lorcan's decision to drop out of university and go travelling but when they saw the state he was in they said nothing and took him in. He lived at his parent's home for six months and recovered what he himself freely admitted was a fairly loose grip on reality. He could not bear to be in a room with more than two or three people and the noise of even the small town in which he lived left him breathless and ready to flee. During a visit north Eoghan told him that he was now a manager in the government department south of the border which looked after the state's mountains, forests and boglands and he said he would try to get Lorcan a position. It was a gift and gave him the solitude which he craved although he continued to be pestered by the demons of his mind for many years.

He spent most of his working days out in the open air, logging birds and mammals, planting trees and shrubs and building dry stone walls. The house that came with the job sat on the side of a narrow-track of a road, miles from the nearest town. Lorcan had a push bike and once a week cycled to a country shop for supplies. The shop keeper and a manager who came to visit him once a month were almost the only people that Lorcan ever saw during the years that he lived there.

Lorcan had been brought up as Catholic, although it was religion that he now shied away from. He found more comfort in eastern philosophies than in western Christianity but still was unable to commit himself totally to a single doctrine. He had come to the conclusion that most religions were based on genuine mystical insights which, depending on how far you wanted to go, came from either the outer limits of the human psyche or, if you were prepared to go a bit further, beyond the psyche. Instinctively he felt that the LSD he had taken had opened his mind to the areas where those insights originated and that the chink through which he had peered had still not been properly sealed. It was in this zone of the psyche where prophets and mystics believed they came in contact with gods and experienced nirvana. However, the human mind could not deal with the purely abstract messages being sent from these regions and so had to describe what it was experiencing or perceiving by using symbols. Lorcan felt it was when these symbols became doctrine and were encompassed into a religious ritual that problems arose. With time, he came to grudgingly appreciate the unique insights that he had been given. He had seen aspects of the psyche denied to most people but which clearly existed and no matter how unnerving, and at times frightening, it was an area of his mind that he felt he should force himself to return to and discover what he could about himself. During his years of solitude he sent off for books on psychology and philosophy as well as western and eastern mysticism and took comfort from the fact that others had gone through what he had to different degrees, often much more severe than what had happened to him. These were often instigated by the intake of some external stimulant but were also the result of a flaw in the psyche, attributed to some sort of mystical insight by those whose minds had been affected. Lorcan believed that it was those areas of the unconscious that are normally only accessed by dreams or people who believe that they are gaining mystical insights that had been opened to him by the LSD he had taken.

17

FOLLOWING HIS BREAK UP WITH KEI, Wolf spent more time than ever at various protests, particularly in South America and the Antarctic where he became almost an associate member of Selva Global. Kei was as good as her word and he was able to develop a reasonable relationship with his daughter. When he was barred from entering the US because of his participation in protests against US-owned companies in the Amazon and Antarctic, Kei went out of her way to travel from her new home in New York with Irinda to ensure that father and daughter were able to spend time together. Wolf and Kei developed a cordial relationship but it was a tense one that left both of them edgy.

Wolf was a late comer to technology and the idea for the ecopunks website came from Niels. He had seen the early potential of the internet as a means for individual activists and groups from around the world to swap information and highlight the campaigns that they were involved in. Wolf agreed to write an occasional piece for the site, reporting on the campaigns he was involved in and giving it a hands-on feel. Niels spent hours uploading information and images and creating graphics and hyperlinks. Initially the site was unwieldy with millions of words of information but Neil began to patiently wade through this and edited it down into more manageable components that catered to everyone from the merely curious who wanted some snappy and easily digestible piece of information about a particular environmental issue or concern to more detailed statistics and analysis. So engrossed was he in his work that Niels did not notice for a full week that Sophie and their children had moved out of their apartment and in with a 20-year-old Danish activist who had only become an ecopunks associate the previous year. Although he made a fuss he later told Wolf that he was secretly relieved and Niels and Sophie maintained an amicable relationship.

The ecopunks website became one of the most visited environmental resources on the world wide web but Niels wanted to give it a personality and make it an easily identifiable brand. He eventually persuaded Wolf to spend more time in Amsterdam and become its de facto editor, freeing Niels up to work on the technical side of things and the overall appearance. Technology was advancing and he was now able to incorporate video clips and sound elements into the site.

Given that Niels, Wolf and Sophie had hovered on the fringes of alternative society for most of their lives and that Wolf and Sophie in separate ways were almost figureheads for some elements it was inevitable that they attracted a broad left-of-centre audience. Wolf provided the seasoned activist edge to it, advising on how to set up protests, drum up community support and to lobby elected representatives. The site also flagged up campaigns from around the world and Wolf used his editorial blogs to draw together the various strands and put small, apparently parochial issues into a global context.

Sophie's input focused on alternative ecofriendly technologies and included advice on building everything from wind-turbines from old washing machine parts to houses made from clay and wattle, growing organic vegetables and advice for ensuring that children being brought up on a vegetarian diet received the right proteins and nutrients.

Other contributors gave medical advice ranging from acupuncture, herbal remedies and aromatherapy. Exercise regimes were based on yoga, Tai Chi or other non-violent martial arts. As well as being an environmental news resource the ecopunks website became a lifestyle accessory for many people.

After spending six months in Amsterdam working nearly every day with Niels and Sophie to build up the content and feel of the website Wolf decided to take a break with his then girlfriend Ana. She was a devotee of the mystic philosopher Sri Aurobindo and suggested a six-week trip to an ashram in Pondicherry in south east India. Wolf was glad of the opportunity to drop out of sight for a while and hitched a lift on a boat sailing to Mumbai before making his way overland to Pondicherry where he and Ana had booked into the ashram.

He attended lectures and meditation classes every day and lived on a diet of dhal and chapattis. Yet it was difficult for him to conform to the discipline required, not to mention Ana's insistence on taking separate rooms and a regime of sexual-abstinence during their stay. While he could understand the philosophy of what he was hearing and began to unwind during the meditation he suspected that any insights into his own psyche would only come during the act of living and that these would not emerge as a sudden revelation but over time and with hindsight. This was of course almost a manifesto for continuing to live the life that he had been to date and Wolf acknowledged that there was an element of self-justification.

However, the ashram did give him an opportunity for reflection, the first time he had sat still for long enough to take stock of where he had come from, what he had become and where he saw himself going. He was now in his mid-thirties and was tiring of the dreadlocked hippy image that he felt had almost made him into a living cliché. He asked Ana to shave his head and the long goatee beard he had grown and when he emerged from the ashram, having mutually agreed with Ana to call off their now entirely celibate relationship, to make his way back to the Netherlands he had also abandoned the three pairs of combat trousers and collection of tie-dye tee-shirts that he had arrived in India with for a pair of dark jeans and a black hemp shirt.

18

SUSPICIONS HAD LONG BEEN CIRCULATING AMONG environmentalists that there was a link between some elements of the scientific community and large mining corporations. This was reinforced when an expedition to an isolated part of a South American rain forest was followed a year or two later by an application for a zinc mining licence by a company called AKNR. The Argentinean group Selva Global got word of what was happening and set up a protest and began to lobby their various contacts to highlight it. However, the regional government backed the mining scheme saying that it would bring employment opportunities to an impoverished and isolated region. The indigenous people of the area were brought on board and the protesters were forced to back off. A decade later the mining company had stripped several square miles of rain forest, dug up huge craters, poisoned the soil and water supply with acids and made redundant their locally employed workforce, who never numbered more than 100 anyway and who worked as manual labourers.

The mining company had carried out further surveys in the region throughout the ten-year period it operated there but were unable to find any further 'economically viable' mineral deposits. Selva Global activists began to ask how AKNR had discovered the lucrative deposit in the first place and learned that an international scientific expedition had been in the area a year before the mining license was applied for. It had included sociologists who studied the indigenous people – their culture and language – botanists, zoologists and, significantly, a geologist who took numerous soil samples and drilled out core samples at depths not normally associated with such expeditions. The expedition leaders passed it off as an indication of their thoroughness. However, a seed of doubt was sown. When the Selva Global researchers sought out the reports of the expedition published in various scientific journals they were unsurprised at the brevity of the geological section and the half-hearted attempts by the report's author, Marco Torres, to tie it into the other areas of expertise.

Torres's name was noted and they began to look into other expeditions he had taken part in and saw a pattern. He always seemed to work in the remotest regions and with expeditions that had the biggest budgets. The cost of sending a scientific team and transporting its equipment to remote area was prohibitive and in particularly the heavy drilling equipment that geologists used to take core samples. But the expeditions on which Torres went were always carried out on behalf of G8 governments or major universities and had a higher-than-normal level of financial backing. Over a period of 11 years Selva Global discovered that Torres had taken part in more than 15 such expeditions and that within a year mining licences on behalf AKNR had been applied for in locations where at least six of them had taken place, half of which subsequently proved to be economically viable and which were open-pit mined and abandoned in just a few years when all but the most inaccessible deposits had been plundered. Selva Global had contacted Niels at the ecopunks website and asked him to help highlight the issue and he agreed. However, Niels decided he could take things a stage further and started trying to hack into AKNR's computer. It took him two weeks but he was rewarded with detailed discussions between senior executives identifying where planned scientific expeditions were due to take place and which ones were going to areas which were believed to have mineral resources. The company's operation was global and its influence went way beyond what Selva Global had suspected.

There was a series of correspondence between the organisers of an expedition to Alaska to study the migration habits of caribou and the impact upon their breeding patterns of changes to the environment caused by global warming. The scientific team had identified an area through which the majority of caribou seemed to migrate, however, the vice-chancellor of the university – whose background was in economics – was urging them to split their study into two areas, including one which was some 30 kilometres away from where the caribou passed. When his reasoning was queried he suggested that it could help establish why the animals chose one route rather than another and if the geological make-up of the routes was a factor. When the scientific rationale behind this was in turn queried the vice-chancellor replied curtly that unless his request was acceded to funding for the expedition would be withdrawn. Niels also found on the AKNR archives a document highlighting a potential mineral deposit in the area where the vice-chancellor had requested the expedition to investigate and a memo to the company's accountant authorising a six-figure payment to an account in a Caribbean-based bank in the name of the university vice-chancellor. Another memo said that 'MT' had been assigned to the project. Niels immediately hacked in to the AKNR's personnel department and a quick search of the files there revealed that one of the best-paid members of staff was Marco Torres, although he was not attached to any particular department and access to information on his employment record was restricted to the director in charge of personnel. Despite Neils' best efforts he was unable to obtain any more information. However, he was quickly able to establish that AKNR were major contributors to some of the most powerful governments in the world and also made donations to major universities in Europe and the US. From the correspondence he uncovered it was clear that they were not afraid to use their contacts to ensure that their personnel were given places on their scientific teams.

When Wolf returned from his retreat in India he felt rested and was ready to reveal his new shaven-headed ecophilosopher persona to the world. After a morning of oohing and head-slapping Wolf, Niels and Sophie settled down to discuss developments and bring Wolf up to date with campaigns that they were ready to launch on the ecopunks site and requests from other groups asking for Wolf's involvement.

'This is dynamite,' said Niels excitedly punching up the presentation he had had put together on AKNR and the role of Torres. He had obtained video footage from Selva Global of the scarred landscape of one of their mining projects and photographs of the company's senior executives standing alongside senior politicians. Using images, graphics, text and sinister ambient music that he had composed himself Niels had created a mini-web documentary lasting for just over three-minutes exposing AKNR staff piggy-backing along with respected scientific expeditions to remote parts of the planet, incurring minimal costs for themselves and gaining access to isolated and often protected areas. The documentary then highlighted three instances where a year or so after these expeditions, exploration licenses were applied for, correspondence sent to governments urging that protections be lifted in return for international funding – or in one case the withdrawal of funding – to allow AKNR to start mining.

Niels watched Wolf excitedly as his documentary played.

'We can go live on this any time,' he said. 'And there is material for a full hour-long documentary which we could make ourselves and distribute to alternative and left-of-centre TV networks. You can front them Wolf. It is perfect for the new direction we want to go in.'

Wolf sat silently contemplating the photo of Marco Torres which was still on the screen.

'Are you going to highlight his role?' he said at last.

'Absolutely he is key to the whole thing,' said Niels. 'He is the link between AKNR and the scientific expeditions. I know we will be making a fall guy of someone who is being paid to do a job rather than those who are making the real profits but we need to do this to flush the big guys out.'

Wolf sighed.

'What's wrong, Wolf?' asked Sophie. 'Do you know him?'

'That's Kei's new partner.'

'Fuck!' exclaimed Niels.

'He's Peruvian, right?' said Sophie.

'I think he has US citizenship as well?' said Wolf.

'You can't be personal about this and worry about Kei,' insisted Niels.

'Oh come on, Niels,' said Sophie. 'What about Irinda? How long to you think it would take someone to cop on that this guy we are targeting is bringing up Wolf's daughter? Given what you have just told us about AKNR they are unscrupulous enough to

123

hang out their own employees to dry to take the spotlight off them.'

'Shit that fucker is with Kei,' he said. 'Maybe she doesn't know?'

'Doesn't care more like,' said Sophie. 'You know Kei … 'you live your life and I'll live mine you don't try to impose your values on me and I'll not impose mine on you'.

Wolf sighed.

'That about sums her up … but I'll go and talk to her and at least see if she realises what he has been doing,' he said.

'What should I tell the Selva Global people?' said Niels. 'This is a big deal for them.'

'I'll have to be honest with Kei and tell her that we are going to expose Marco and his company,' said Wolf.

'That could scupper everything,' sighed Niels.

'It's worth a try. She might even let me take Irinda back here for a few months until the fuss has died down,' Wolf said. 'Kei may not share our ideals but she does respect them. Get everything ready to roll and if I suspect that Kei is going to squeal I'll let you know and we can go public but I'll just have to keep a low profile on this one.'

Wolf had often editorialised on the ecopunks website about the huge growth in air travel as airlines became more competitive and ticket prices fell. Planes burned enormous amounts of fuel and the emissions from a single aeroplane in its working life would have a measurable impact on the earth's atmosphere. Yet he was conscious that many people who would otherwise support sustainable energy policies would be reluctant to abandon air travel. Wolf was in many ways in a privileged position, he could usually hitch a lift on a small boat or ship sailing to whatever part of the world he wanted to travel but that was through a network of contacts and because of a profile that most travellers did not have. How could Wolf stand and eulogise the beauty and tranquillity of an Indonesian rainforest, an African jungle or the fragile ecosystem of the Antarctic and deny other people the opportunity of experiencing it by urging them not to travel by the only realistically method of getting there? The moral argument was clear cut but society had got to such a stage that time was now corralled and that most people's travel itinerary was restricted to a few weeks when they had to get from one part of the world to another in the quickest possible time. Wolf had tried to rationalise the debate by arguing that air travel was probably inevitable but that people should at least try to ration it and where possible use other means of transport and support reforestation projects to offset the carbon emissions generated by their journey. He had on occasion travelled by plane himself when no other means was possible and on one occasion been photographed at an airline check-in desk and vilified by the media and other environmental activists as a hypocrite. Sophie and Niels seemed slightly taken aback when he told them that he was travelling to New York by plane, but had not criticised him as he half expected and Sophie accompanied him to the airport.

'In a way its good you haven't gone public with his new baldy image of yours,' Sophie said glancing round nervously in case anyone should recognise Wolf despite his makeover. 'But how are you going to get past the US immigration officials? Surely your name is going to set their computer klaxons blaring.'

'Sometimes it is better not to know these things because they will only land you in trouble,' said Wolf.

'Don't you patronise me.' retorted Sophie.

'Fair enough ... but a man is entitled to keep a few trade secrets about himself.'

'Dodgy passports can land you in prison.'

'Who said it is dodgy,' smiled Wolf waving a maroon EU passport in front of her.

He had already purchased his ticket online and as he approached the check-in desk Sophie, despite her curiosity, walked away and let him check-in in private.

'There is really no chance that Kei will let you take Irinda back here is there?' said Sophie when Wolf came back over to her.

He shrugged.

'You know something I have never mentioned,' he continued.

'What?'

'All my ideological objections to air travel have also been a convenient cover to the fact that I am absolutely shit-scared of flying.'

'What Mr Macho ecowarrior?' laughed Sophie.

But Wolf was genuinely trembling. He had spent weeks living 30-metres above ground in a tree, dangled from cliff edges with a camera to show the damage done by egg collectors to a white-tailed eagle nest and even climbed some of the more accessible slopes of the Himalayas to highlight the disappearance of glaciers. On a couple of occasions he had flown in helicopters and light aircraft to film the extent of deforestation in the Amazon, or how sea levels were threatening to swamp a Polynesian island. Height and flying as such did not bother him, however, the long-tube cabins of passenger jumbo jets left him feeling claustrophobic with a knot of anxiety in his stomach and a crushing pain in his chest that he feared might be an oncoming heart attack. He always had an almost irresistible urge to flee before the cabin doors were locked. That was just when the plane was on the runway and his panic did not abate until he was staggering from the plane into the terminal building at the end of the journey.

Wolf caught a bus from JFK into Manhattan and then managed

to navigate his way on the city's underground to the address that Kei had sent him. He had spent the flight trying to articulate what he would say, running lines over and over again like a mantra, as much to take his mind off the mid-Atlantic turbulence as to embed the words in his mind. He was jet-lagged and in the delicate twilight zone between drunkenness and the onslaught of a hangover, having downed half a dozen mini-bottles of whiskey on the flight in an effort to numb his fear. He knew he should check in to a hostel or try to contact some of his associates to secure a bed for the night before confronting Kei and Marco but now that he was there he was keen to see Irinda. The address he had been given was in mid-town Manhattan in a tall town house and without trying to think too much about what was going to happen next Wolf rang the door bell. He was surprised when Marco answered almost immediately.

'Ah hello Wolf, at last. Did you have a good flight?' he said.

Wolf felt uneasy.

'Hello Marco. Is Irinda here?'

'Come on in?'

Wolf tried to tell himself that his paranoia was being driven by a combination of jetlag and the hangover that was starting to kick in, as well as a natural apprehension about meeting his daughter and ex-wife. Despite his misgivings he followed Marco into the hallway and through to a small sitting room where, with a pang of anguish, he saw a photograph hanging on the wall of Marco with Irinda on his shoulders and Kei nestling into him.

Marco followed his gaze and nodded to him to take a seat.

'Do you want a drink?' he asked Wolf.

Although he was thirsty Wolf shook his head for he wanted to get out of the house as quick as possible.

'Is Irinda here?' Wolf asked again.

'No,' replied Marco. 'She and her mother left this morning. They should be somewhere over the Pacific Ocean by now on their way to Japan.'

Wolf tried to readjust to cope with this surprise piece of information and profound disappointment that he would not now get to see his daughter.

'Was it planned?' he asked.

'I suggested it this morning when I heard you were coming and Kei immediately agreed. We didn't tell Irinda.'

'Any point in asking how you knew I was coming?' asked Wolf glancing around him and wondering if he should make a run for it before anyone else arrived on the scene.

'Your hacker friend in Amsterdam, Mr Lunnig, has been leaving his cyberprints all over my employer's mainframe and so they returned the courtesy and hacked back in. You used your friend's computer to book your flights to New York and so we guessed you would come to see Kei before going public with your alleged findings about me.'

'Did you tell Kei what was happening?'

'I didn't have much choice. You know her as well as I do … can you imagine trying to tell her that she should take off with her daughter for an unspecified period of time without giving her a good reason?'

'So you told her that you had been infiltrating supposed scientific expeditions to gain access to remote, environmentally sensitive areas to identify mineral and oil deposits without incurring suspicion or expensive exploration costs.'

'Jesus … you really do talk like that … I thought you eco guys just came out with sound bites when you were speaking on the television.'

'Quit fucking about. Did you tell her?' demanded Wolf.

'Not in such pretentious or judgmental language.'

'And what did she say.'

'Oh she was pissed off all right. To an extent she does share your values but not to the point where she thought you would ever expose herself and Irinda to the spotlight.'

'I'm not planning that. I came to tell Kei what was happening and to get off side before we go live with the information we have on you. It looks like she has done that anyway.'

'Ah,' sighed Marco. 'When was exactly were you due to go live?'

'There is no 'was' about it, it will go ahead.'

'Listen Wolf I don't think you realise how naive you and your friends are being. I don't want to come out with clichés and say you don't know who you are messing with ... but you really don't. These guys don't piss around.'

'Is that a threat?'

'I don't need to do that Wolf. Look at you trembling, you must know now that you have been tracked from Europe all the way across the Atlantic. I can even tell you what brand of whiskey you had to drink on the plane and what you had for dinner. We've even worked out how many tonnes of carbon fuel were burned to get you here to go into the press release we will issue to counter your propaganda. We've got quite a sizeable portfolio on you now. Lots of people get paranoid and think that they are being watched ... well you have more justification than most.'

'My colleagues know I am here. I left details with them.'

Marco sighed and Wolf thought he detected a look of weariness on his face.

'Don't worry you'll walk out of here alive and be allowed to go wherever you want, probably ... just keep an eye over you shoulder.'

'Surely your bosses are going to be a bit fucked off if they ever find out that you are telling me all this.'

'Oh they already know ... they're listening in to every word.'

'Has Kei gone to her parents' home?' asked Wolf moving towards the door.

'Yes,' said Marco.

'We'll release the information we have on you today.'

'I hope your colleague has got lots of money to buy a new computer system because I think that what you just said was the signal to launch a virus that will wipe out your computer's hard drive as well as that of your service provider. The virus will also target your subscribers, advertisers and any regular users. I say it has already happened and anyone who is offline at present will be infected next time they go online. Any back up information that you saved has already been infected so I would advise you not to use any discs that have been near your computer system in the last five weeks.'

Wolf's first instinct was to phone Niels when he was back on the street but as he switched on his mobile a message came on to his screen to say that his sim card had been wiped and that he was no longer able to access any networks. He looked over his shoulder and saw a car pulling out from beside Marco's house and driving slowly along the street behind him. Across on the opposite pavement a man was making a very bad pretence of reading a newspaper while leaning against a lamp post. Wolf concluded he wasn't even pretending. He wanted to sleep but did not want to compromise any of his contacts in New York, though he suspected that their identity would be no big mystery to those who were following him, and instead began to make his way back to the airport and jump on the first flight to any airport with a 200km radius of Amsterdam.

Marco had not overstated the damage that the virus would do for as well as destroying all of Neil's computer equipment it engendered a blame game among many environmental groups, activists and individuals who had no more than a passing interest in the environment and whose equipment was infected and also destroyed. A raft of legal writs ensured that no-one was ever allowed to say publicly that the mining company AKNR was even suspected of being behind the virus. It took six months to set up a new ecopunks website for as well as the need to obtain new equipment many service providers were reluctant to host the site in case it was targeted again. For the same reason when the site was eventually up and running it was a no-go area for many people.

There was an upside – there was a huge buzz among computer nerds, geeks and professionals about the cyberbomb and Niels was inundated with offers from people keen to do an autopsy on his hardware and help him build a firewall and series of failsafes that would ensure the new site and its users would never be left as vulnerable again.

Wolf had been involved in environmental campaigning for more than 15 years and had suffered numerous physical assaults and demonisation. He been forced to face the possibility of his own imminent demise on at least four occasions but nothing had ever undermined his confidence as that confrontation with Marco Torres. When he arrived back in Amsterdam he phoned Kei and had a brief and frosty conversation with her before a totally one-side chat with his shy daughter. When Kei came back on Wolf said he wanted to meet on a one-to-one basis.

'You will have to come here,' said Kei.

'No problem, although you realise that Marco's employers are probably listening to this conversation and will follow me when I get there,' replied Wolf.

Kei was silent for a few seconds.

'Marco told me that our relationship is over,' she said. 'He is packaging up our stuff and sending it to me in Nagoya. I am going to stay here for a while until I get my life together. I have rented a house already.'

Wolf was stunned and saddened for his former wife and for Irinda who was bound to find the change of countries and language upsetting as well as the sudden loss of a man who, Wolf had to admit, had probably been quite a good stepfather to her. He told Kei he would travel of Nagoya and for the third time in less than a week he found himself preparing to undertake a lengthy flight. He tried to remember the meditation techniques that he had learned during his time in India for he felt he was teetering on the edge of a nervous breakdown and only the thought of seeing his daughter forced him to get on the plane.

Kei and Irinda met him at the airport and both were distant, Irinda had not seen her father for nearly six months. As they left the airport Wolf saw the man who had been leaning against the lamppost in New York standing with a shoulder bag. He didn't even pretend to be surreptitious and waved over.

'Who is that?' asked Kei.

'I first saw him outside your and Marco's house in New York,' said Wolf. 'I also think I may have seen him when I was walking in the Vondelpark in Amsterdam yesterday, although that was more a case of catching a glance of him out of the corner of my eye before he turned a corner.'

Kei took out a mobile phone, dialled and walked away and left Wolf and Irinda to shyly talk to one another. As she came back Wolf heard another phone ringing and turned to see his stalker answer his. The man frowned as he listened and then nodded before turning and walking back in to the airport without looking towards Wolf or Kei.

'Relax, Wolf. They are just trying to freak you out,' said Kei.

'They're doing a good job,' sighed Wolf.

'Tell Wolf about your new school, Irinda,' said Kei.

Irinda took Wolf by the hand and started chatting excitedly while her mother hailed a taxi.

At Kei's new house they ate and when the little girl went to bed she insisted that both her parents come and read her a story. When she was asleep Kei and Wolf sat down with a bottle of wine and for what Wolf suspected was going to be a serious chat.

'I'll say what I have to and then that is the end of it until you go home,' said Kei.

'Fair enough.'

'I can't say that I would have stayed with Marco for ever, it had become more platonic than a proper relationship, but I feel your threat to name him in your campaign has forced the whole issue. That is why I blame you ... not so much because your actions ended the relationship but because once again you have forced me to alter a way of living that I was quite comfortable with.'

'Marco was prepared to see you and Irinda named to distract attention away from the campaign we were about to launch.'

'His employers were. Marco is as scared of them as you are. He actually admires you – in a begrudging sort of way. I tried to put him right and tell him what a self-righteous wanker you can be.'

'Thanks.'

'Marco told me to leave and it was his idea that we should stay here. I don't think it is what he wants but he knows that his employers will use Irinda and me if you or any other environmental group tries to cause trouble for his company again. I can't accept that and that is why I have agreed. That is why I am pissed off at you.'

'Can't he leave AKNR and come and work here?' Wolf forced himself to ask, although following the clinical conversation he'd had with Marco he could not believe that the geologist was so noble as Kei was implying.

'I told you he is afraid of them.'

'But he has more influence than you would like me to think. How come you were able to phone him and tell to call off that goon who was following me?' demanded Wolf.

'I didn't phone Marco?'

'Who then?'

'It doesn't matter.'

Kei glared at Wolf and he sensed he was on dangerous territory but he was determined to persist, even if it meant him been thrown out and forced to find somewhere to sleep in a strange city at this hour of the night. He stared back.

'I had an affair with Marco's boss, Hal,' sighed Kei, but her gaze was still defiant. 'I told him if he didn't get his people to back off you I would tell his wife. Hal's father-in-law is the chief executive of AKNR and he can't stand each Hal. One whimper from his daughter and Hal would be out on his ear and probably prosecuted on a trumped up charge of embezzlement.'

'Does Marco know?'

'No.'

Wolf took a sip of wine.

PART THREE

19

FROM THE WAY THE VAN WAS slowing down and starting up again Wolf knew that they were in Ljubljana and driving through the city's traffic. He gripped Madja's hand, as much to reassure himself as her. When the van stopped it was several minutes before the door swung open and the two guards who had sat inside with them motioned for them to move forward. As Wolf stepped out he was greeted with a roar of anger and he had to duck as a bottle was hurled towards his head and smashed against the door of the van in which he had been travelling. He felt his head being pushed down by policemen on either side of him as he was rushed towards the entrance of a building and away from the hostile crowd. Madja came behind him. They were taken to a room with a video surveillance camera on the wall and a number of chairs on either side of a desk and told to sit. Two guards stayed in the room with them.

'My God,' exclaimed Madja. 'What have those people been told? You would think that we had killed that poor man.'

'It's more a case of what they have not been told,' sighed Wolf.

'All they know is that an innocent man is dead and that we are somehow implicated in that.'

'But he was cutting down the trees … I mean I know that is no reason for him to die but he was part of what was going on and it was one of his own side who shot him.'

'You and I can say that but we don't know what the security guards are saying. They will probably try to concoct some story to cover for their colleague and unless it is watertight it will start to come apart. Now, that won't happen tonight or tomorrow and in the meantime we have to just sit tight and when you are questioned tell them exactly what happened, at the worst you might be prosecuted for trespass.'

'But that is no reason to keep someone in prison for two or three days.'

'Given what is going on out there this might be the best place for us.'

Wolf was taken to a cell and surprised himself by falling into a deep, dreamless sleep from which he did not wake until the morning when a policeman brought him in orange juice, coffee and warm bread rolls. From somewhere outside he could hear a cellist practising a scale and then what he thought was a piece by Bach. As prisons went this was one of the better ones he had been in, mused Wolf. He finished his breakfast and did some push-ups and stretches and tried to steel himself for the day ahead. He could hear doors rattling and other snippets of music from somewhere nearby. Finally the cell door opened and the policeman who had brought him breakfast motioned to him.

'Where does the music come from?' asked Wolf as he stepped out.

'There is a conservatoire next door,' replied the policeman. 'If it annoys you there are cells on the other side of the building that are quieter.'

Wolf shook his head and smiled ruefully at the cop's casual assumption that he would be staying at the police station for some time. Wolf was brought to an interview room and was greeted by Gustav Linser, who in his younger days had squatted with the other members of the ecopunks collective in Amsterdam before training as a solicitor. He had represented Wolf and other activists in various courtrooms throughout Europe.

'Another fine mess Wolf,' he muttered as the policeman took up his position in a corner.

'They haven't actually questioned me yet,' said Wolf.

'From the media reports I don't think there is too much they can hang you for. The problem that I can see it that whatever the go for they they will go for it big time. You'll get out on bail, probably not that much because it will be linked to the seriousness of the charge, but I suspect there will be strict conditions and you will have to surrender your passport to stop you leaving the jurisdiction.'

'How long until it goes to trial?'

'Not overly long, five or six months,' said Gustav. 'But I have contacted a few legal colleagues here in Ljubljana the consensus is that because you will not go down for anything – maybe a fine – the only way you can be punished is by making sure you do not leave the country for as long as possible. An editorial in one of the morning newspapers has actually said that.'

'Can we not argue that it would be dangerous ... that I could be attacked?'

'Absolutely and I have no doubt that the police will offer you secure accommodation – not in a prison as such, but somewhere where your movements would be severely restricted. Purely for your own safety you understand.'

Wolf was silent as he tried to weigh up his options.

'So what is the public mood?'

'The press is divided, but only in the sense of the degree of your culpability. Some are blaming you directly for Mr Dolar's death, others are less judgmental but making the point that if you had not been there he would still be alive.'

'What about Madja, any comments on her?'

'A naive teenagers who got caught up in events. Some reports haven't even mentioned that she was there.'

'And the politicians.'

'Universal condemnation of your irresponsible actions. Even normally ecofriendly politicians are accusing you of hijacking a perfectly legitimate campaign for your own, undefined obviously, agenda.'

Wolf sighed, although he was not surprised.

'Oh well. Lets get the questioning out of the way first and take it from there,' he said looking towards the policeman.

After a few minutes a more senior policeman arrived along with a translator and a Slovenian solicitor who had been engaged by Gustav to advise on any points of the country's law that arose. The questioning lasted little more than half an hour and ended after Gustav suggested that the policeman was merely repeating earlier questions. As they expected later that afternoon Wolf was charged with trespass and, to his surprise, assaulting a security guard during his dash to the forest. He was taken to a court where the charges were put to him and on the advice of his Slovenian solicitor he pleaded guilty to the charge of trespass and was fined 300 euro on the spot.

'Sneaky bastards,' said Gustav. 'They must have known that would happen and threw in the assault charge to make sure you didn't walk.'

'Can I not just plead guilty on that one as well and pay the fine?' asked Wolf.

'Too risky. Assault is a jailable offence, depending of course on the severity and as that hasn't been established yet the prosecution could demand a maximum sentence. Best to contest it and see how things pan out.'

Wolf nodded gloomily and listened uncomprehendingly as his Slovenian solicitor and his prosecution counterpart argued the terms of his bail with the judge. Five thousand euro and a requirement to handover his passport and report to police once a day in Ljubljana was the result that left Wolf stranded in the city for at least the next four weeks and where, given the fact that a number of people in the public gallery had shouted out 'murderer' when he stood to face the charges, he was genuinely concerned for his personal safety.

His solicitors asked for time to sort out an address and he was taken back to the police station where he was returned to the same cell where he had spent the previous night, although the door was not locked. Wolf's mobile phone, which had been taken from him following his arrest was returned to him and he phoned Sophie in Amsterdam to arrange for the fine and bail lodgement to be paid. She told him that she was using their network of contacts to try and find a secure address where he could stay until his next court appearance.

'Can you come down here? I want you to bring a few things,' said Wolf.

'Give me a few days until I get a baby sitter organised. By the way your friend Madja emailed, she has been released into her parents' custody. Her friend has brought round your laptop and camera and Madja wants to come and visit you?'

The next day Gustav arrived with a Slovenian avant-garde artist called Jelka, who Wolf immediately suspected was looking for a bit of outlaw kudos, and who offered Wolf a set of rooms in an outhouse on her property, which was located on the edge of the city.

'Can we trust her to keep quiet while I am there?' muttered Wolf to Gustav.

His lawyer nodded.

'She was quite up front and will sell her story after you have left, but will say nothing until then. So try not to get too involved with her unless you want lurid details about the your sexual prowess, or lack of it, splashed across the pages of some gossip mag.'

'I thought you said she was married.'

'She is,' replied Gustav. 'To an actor, who is an even bigger publicity seeker than she is and who would probably be quite happy to play the role of tragic cuckold for a well-paid front-page splash.'

20

WOLF AND THE POLICE AGREED THAT he would leave the police station in the early hours of the morning to ensure there were as few people around as possible and that he would be given a discreet escort. The police officer who brought him his evening meal said there were a dozen protestors outside the station holding placards and demanding that he should be jailed for murder.

'I recognise some of them, they are serial protesters and next week will probably be demonstrating about lax immigration laws or taxes on property,' the policeman said. 'There are a couple of student types there as well and I wouldn't be surprised if they were being paid to be there.'

Wolf nodded, he had seen such scenarios before. Businesses who were being targeted by environmental campaigners often orchestrated their own counter demonstrations to suggest that there was popular support for what they were doing – often couched in terms of employment opportunities or financial benefits to the areas in which they were working. However, those who were paid to stand on such picket lines were unlikely to cause too much trouble, they were not paid to get themselves arrested. As agreed Jelka arrived at the police station at around 4am and told Wolf that there were a couple of people still standing outside who looked more bored than angry.

'Let's go for it then,' said Wolf nodding to the policeman on duty. Jelka had parked her car right beside the entrance and they were inside and driving away before the protesters even stirred although Wolf saw one of them frantically dialling on a mobile phone. The city streets were quiet apart from Jelka's car and the unmarked police vehicle that followed, Wolf kept looking to see in case another vehicle should join their convoy but saw none. It took just over half an hour driving through the suburbs of Ljubljana to what appeared to be the countryside, although Jelka assured Wolf that they were still within the city limits as specified in his bail conditions. The houses here seemed to be set well apart from one another and when Jelka turned from the road a set of automatic gates set in a high brick wall swung open to let them through and then closed again behind them. Wolf lifted his bags from the back seat and was taken by Jelka into the main house, which was dimly lit and which he took little notice off, through a patio and into a huge garden with a number of outbuildings.

'That one over there is my studio,' said Jelka pointing. 'I will be there working for most of the day if you need me and then I can take you to the police station in the evening – your solicitor said we could go to one near here instead of in the city – to report to police.'

Jelka led Wolf up a few steps and pushed open a wooden door to a small apartment, pointing out a kitchenette, bathroom and bedroom. 'I have left a list of phone numbers beside the phone if you need me,' she said. Wolf nodded his thanks and slumped down onto a sofa beside an open window and looked into the darkness beyond. It took a few minutes for his eyes to discern the shape of a river flowing just below him.

The death of Eric Dolar still depressed Wolf and he re-ran the scene constantly in his mind. This was not the first time that his activities and those of fellow protesters had been blamed on someone losing their life. Just a year earlier he had taken part in a protest outside a plastics factory in Finland which had surreptitiously been pumping waste into a nearby river causing a huge fish kill and destroying plant and animal life along the river banks. The company denied all responsibility and accused the protesters of endangering hundreds of jobs on which many people in a nearby town depended. It was a hard argument to counter because while the people of the town might have been appalled at the pollution and long-term health risks to themselves and their families, the short-term reality was that they were dependent on the wages generated by the company to pay for their houses, food, education of their children and health care for their elderly. A counter protest was mounted each morning by the wives and children of the predominantly male workforce outside the factory and across the road from where Wolf and his fellow environmental protesters had positioned themselves. This tended to last for half and hour before the children were brought to their schools when most of them dispersed and a handful stayed behind to maintain a small token presence.

Although the majority of those protesting against the factory were not from the region they were nearly all Finnish. However, the presence of Wolf and other international activists had been picked up on by the factory management and its political supporters who accused them of being outsiders interfering in the economic wellbeing of a small town. There had been hostile cat calls between the two groups of protesters with the some of the factory supporters urging the environmentalists to go home and sort out their own countries' problems before preaching to them, while the Finnish campaigners accused their opponents of being racist. A constant police presence kept the two sides apart.

Two or three times per week a convoy of lorries arrived at the factory with raw material and the green protesters would try to block them by pushing through the police lines and lying on the road. Inevitably they would be dragged away by the police and the lorries would be allowed to pass. Like so many protests Wolf had taken part in before, this one also developed its own routines and seemingly inevitable pattern. One morning, however, they were told that a fresh convoy was arriving earlier than predicted and they quickly realised that this had been timed to coincide with the counter protest. Wolf had a bad feeling from the start and told the organisers that they should stand back rather than be drawn in to a direct confrontation. However, the consensus was that if they backed off on this occasion the factory owners would use the same tactic next time.

As the lorries came in to view the green group pushed forward past the police line, which as before had been strengthened in anticipation of the lorries arriving. Normally only a handful of protesters made their way past the police but this time the police line buckled and more than fifty pushed their way through and flung themselves onto the road. The counter-protesting women and children on the other side who on seeing the ecowarriors break through had also pushed forward and begun shouting at them with one or two trying to drag the protestors off the road. Wolf, as one of the most recognisable of the environmentalists had been surrounded by a dozen women, some clutching children, who shouted in Finnish at him with one middle-aged woman constantly poking him the chest while the child she held kept slapping his bald head. Wolf had to restrain himself from laughing at the comedy of the whole thing when he heard the belching horn of one of the lorries and screeching brakes followed by screams.

Two were killed, a 70-year-old male environmental protester from Turku and a 23-year-old mother of two who had tried to push him out of harms way when she saw the lorry approaching too fast and realised that it would be unable to stop in time. The factory owners issued a statement blaming the environmental protesters for the tragedy. However, there was an unexpected outcome to the protest. The husband of the dead woman worked in the factory and told reporters that he had been called before a disciplinary panel for accidentally discharging chemical waste into the river. He said the only reason no action was taken against him was because it would confirm what the environmentalists had been claiming all along. In a bitter tirade in front of a local TV news crew he blamed himself for his wife's death saying that if he had told her the truth about what had happened she would never have joined the counter protest.

In 20 years of campaigning it was one of the rare outright victories for environmental campaigners that Wolf had ever seen. The company's management were fired and a new team brought in who immediately invested in new equipment that drastically reduced the amount of toxic waste that the factory produced. They also set up a fund to restock the river with fish and maintain its surrounding banks. The cost of that success was of course two human lives and Wolf was horrified at what had happened and the less than subtle celebrations of some of those who had taken part in the protest. That was why when Alenka had made her comment about gaining a martyr a few days earlier in the Slovenian forest that he had been so shocked. He didn't actually believe that, but the thought had entered his head that the only way to stop what was happening was for someone to die and ensuring that the subsequent recriminations would force the developers to stop work.

Madja arrived the following day with Wolf's camera and laptop and he brought her to the little balcony in his apartment which overlooked the river.

'So how have you been?' he asked.

'A minor celebrity,' she said. 'Even my parents are impressed.'

'They don't blame you in some way for Erik Dolar's death?'

'Unfortunately you seem to be the one taking most of the flak for that, not from everyone but it has been said by politicians and the company responsible for building the road.'

Wolf shrugged as casually as he could but although he knew that was the situation it was still uncomfortable to hear it.

'Do you get disillusioned?' asked Madja.

'Totally,' replied Wolf, thinking again of Erik Dolar. 'I do genuinely still believe that what we are doing is for the best and that if humanity keeps going on the way it is it will put its very survival at risk. I mean what is the point of a vibrant economy if the very physical nature of the planet metamorphosises into something totally unrecognisable, where agriculture became unsustainable, water undrinkable and temperatures unbearable? Maybe it is hard to relate the destruction of a few hundred trees to such a catastrophe but as I keep saying it is that slow chipping away which was eventually be our undoing and some day there will be nothing left to chip away at.'

'Well at least the destruction of the forest has been put on hold for now,' said Madja.

Wolf was surprised, for no-one had told him this.

'Because of Erik's death?'

Madja shook her head.

'No. When the excavation machinery was moved in to clear the forest floor they started hitting huge rocks in a concentrated area, causing quite a bit of damage to the machinery,' she said. 'Geophysicists were called in to survey the area and they found a series of carved stones set in a circle. It looks like a Neolithic stone circle and the whole project is going to have to be put on hold for at least a year until it is excavated.'

'That is great news,' said Wolf. 'But why was the work not stopped before, or the roadway diverted? I mean surely the developers knew that an archaeological site would have to be excavated before the road would be allowed to go ahead.'

'They didn't know the circle was there until the trees had been cleared and they began to dig three to four metres below the surface.'

'But you said it as a man-made stone circle, which would date it to around three to four thousand years ago, the forest has been there for at least 10,000 years. Humans were still hunter gatherers at that time and would not have had the technology to construct a stone circle ... well, so most historians would tell you.'

'The reports I have seen say it was at a depth that would have taken thousands of years to build up naturally and they are estimating that it must date from around 8,000 BC and probably much earlier? It is all causing a lot of excitement.'

Wolf smiled.

'My ex-wife will be delighted when she hears about this,' he said.

21

KEI SAT BESIDE MARK SHERIFF ON a flight to Paris looking out at where the African coast met the sea. Before they had left Mauritania she had received an anxious phone call from Lorcan telling her that Wolf had been arrested in Slovenia and had been implicated in a man's death. She then had to speak to Irinda, who had seen television footage of her father being dragged off by armed police, and try to placate her. Kei immediately phoned Sophie in Amsterdam. Sophie was able to give a few more details about what had happened and assure her that Wolf had not been directly responsible for anyone's death.

'I've arranged bail for him and found a safe house for him,' Sophie told Kei. 'I plan to travel to Slovenia tomorrow to see him so I should be able to give you a bit more information.'

'Fine I'll call then,' said Kei and immediately phoned back Lorcan to update him on what she knew and to try to reassure Irinda again that her father was in no danger.

'I'll back in Ireland by tomorrow night,' Kei told her.

The journey from Mauritania involved flying to Paris where she and Mark would catch separate flights to Cardiff and Shannon. Mark was reading notes he had taken during the dig and calling up pictures for the structure in the desert on his laptop.

Kei's flicked through the book which she had published in Japan several years ago which outlined the alternative history theories. She had devoted a chapter to the various flood myths. The most obvious exampled was that of Noah's ark and the flood in the Bible but there seem to be echoes of a similar disaster in almost every culture in the world.

According to an Aztec myth there came a great flood in which all mankind was drowned except for a man and his wife called Nota and Nena. In one source it says that 'the water and the sky drew near each other and that all the earth was lost in a single day. The very mountains were swallowed up in the flood, and the waters remained, lying tranquil during fifty and two springs.' But before the flood began, the god Titlachahuan had warned Nota and Nena, to 'hollow a great cypress, into which you shall enter' and they survived the flood. In the Hindu Mahabharatha a man called Manu 'who was endued with great wisdom and devoted to virtue' saw the god Vishnu in the form of a fish while he was washing his hands in a river and Vishnu begged to be saved. Manu put the fish in a jar but it kept getting bigger and bigger, so he put in a tank, then into a river and eventually the ocean. The fish warned Manu of a great flood that would destroy all life and so Manu built a boat for his family and the world's animals. The fish towed the boat to a mountaintop when the flood came and Manu and his family survived. When the flood receded they repopulated the earth.

There were also dozens of flood myths among native North Americans. The Hopi Indians, who live in Arizona, have a myth which tells how they were created by Sotuknang but that their ancestors angered him and that he destroyed the world by fire, and then by cold, but kept recreating it. However, the people of the Earth continued to anger Sotuknang who caused a great flood. The Hopi survived by floating in reeds and eventually came to rest on a small piece of land.

The Masi of east Africa have a legend, very similar to the Biblical story about Noah. It says that God became angry following a murder and resolved to destroy mankind. However, he decided to spare a righteous man call Tumbainot and his family. According to the Masi legend, God ordered Tumbainot to build a wooden ark and take his two wives, six sons and their wives, and some of animals of every sort onboard. A deluge of rain brought a great flood drowning the rest of humanity and the all the beasts. The ark drifted for many weeks and their supplies began to run low. When the rain finally stopped Tumbainot released a dove but when it returned exhausted Tumbainot knew that it had been unable to find a resting place. Several days later he released a vulture and attached an arrow to one of its tail feathers. When the vulture returned that evening without the arrow, Tumbainot reasoned that it must have landed on carrion, and that the flood was receding. Eventually the water began to clear and the ark grounded. Tumbainot saw four rainbows, one in each quarter of the sky, signifying that God's wrath was over.

The Tuvinian of southern Siberia have a myth which tells how a giant turtle supported the earth. However, when it moved it caused the ocean to begin flooding the earth. An old man who had predicted the deluge built a raft and was able to save himself and his family. When the waters receded, the raft was left on a high wooded mountain.

A myth from Lolo in south-western China tells of a god called Tse-gu-dzih who sent a messenger down to earth, asking for some flesh and blood from a mortal. Only one man, Du-mu, complied. In wrath, Tse-gu-dzih locked the rain-gates, and the waters mounted to the sky. Du-mu was saved in a log hollowed out of a Pieris tree, together with his four sons and various animals.

In northern Borneo a folk tale tells how some men went to cut wood for a fence when they found what appeared to be a huge tree trunk lying on the ground. They began to cut it but when blood started to flow they realised that it was a giant snake. They staked it to the ground, killed it, and skinned it before returning home. They held a great feast using the flesh of the snake and made a massive drum from its skin but when they beat the drum it produced no sound. Then in the middle of the night the drum began sounding by itself, calling up a hurricane that came and swept away all the houses, with the people in them. Some were carried out to sea but others survived.

An Australian Aboriginal myth tells how their creator, who was called Bunjil, became angry with his people because of their evil acts. He decided to punish them by urinating into the ocean and causing it to flood. All of humanity was destroyed except those whom Bunjil loved and who he placed in the sky as stars in the sky. A man and a woman who climbed a tall tree on a mountain were the only survivors and it was they who were the ancestors of the human race.

As Kei looked out from the plane at the desert landscape below she suddenly remembered an article she had read on a website and prodded Mark who looked up startled from his notes.

'I've got a theory Mark,' she said, smiling as he groaned.

'What about,' he sighed.

'Well its really hijacking someone else's theory but it could explain the preponderance of flood myths and maybe even how that structure came to be buried beneath the desert.'

'Go on,' said Mark, vaguely interested.

'There are a number of maps dating from the 1500s which appear to show land where the Antarctic ice cap now lies. Twentieth century scientists established that there are two huge islands under the ice and while they are not perfect these maps give a fairly good approximation of their outline,' began Kei.

'Oh come on, Kei,' sighed Mark. 'Don't do this to me, there is no way that the icecaps could not have reached their current depth in just 500 years. It took a million years for them to build up, maybe even longer'

'I'm not suggesting that they are based on the Antarctic landscape of 1512 or whatever, but they could have been copied from much older source material, which in turn may have been based on even older material.'

'Going back a million years?'

'No. Just bear with me. According to a US scientist called Charles Hapgood the ice caps only completely covered the Antarctic 6,000 years ago and the entire continent could have been totally ice free until 13,000 BC.'

'But that flies in the face of science.'

'It all depends on whose science you believe,' said Kei. 'Hapgood, whose theories were backed by Albert Einstein, argued that between those two dates the islands of the Antarctic, may have shifted from a warmer zone into a much colder area.'

'Sure that is possible, but continental drift takes millions of years. Huge land masses do not just simply float off.'

'No, but what Hapgood is talking about is sudden and destructively violent slippage. He argued that the entire Earth's crust was displaced and slid over its inner core causing warmer zones to suddenly end up closer to the north and south poles and become covered by ice within hours. He claims that this is what happened to the Antarctic – that it had previously been in a temperate climate and able to sustain life but was suddenly thrust towards the south pole by displacement of the Earth's crust. Within hours the landscape had frozen and ice dramatically built up over the following centuries to form new polar ice cap. Other areas which had been under ice for hundreds of thousands of years were suddenly hurled in to warmer zones releasing huge volumes of water as the ice melted.'

'How did he come to that conclusion?' demanded Mark.

'In Siberia and Alaska thousands of animals and plants have been found frozen and totally intact with undigested food still in their stomachs. It was as if they had been happily grazing one moment and within a few hours had been frozen to death.'

'Well maybe there was a sudden cold snap and they were caught in a blizzard. It happens all the time.'

'Yes, but they stayed frozen – they are still frozen today in the Arctic Circle. How does a beast grazing in fairly mild grasslands, which depends of fresh shrubs for its diet, suddenly find itself in an environment where the average temperature is minus 40 degrees and the ground is totally covered in ice and snow? Hapgood's theory is that the entire earth's crust is like a skin on the core of the planet and that in certain extreme circumstances it can slip from its existing position.'

Kei folded the palm of her right hand over the fist of her left hand and slid it from side to side to demonstrate the theory.

'The core of the planet remains steady in its angle and orbit around the sun but the outer skin slides to a new position so that London is thrust hundreds of miles south east to where central Africa is and the Finnish part of the Arctic circle follows to end up where Egypt used to be and billions of tonnes of ice suddenly begin to melt. Meanwhile South Africa is pushed closer to the South

Pole and its temperature begins to drop to well below zero, freezing gazelles, wildebeest and lions to death and covering them in the first layer of snow by the following morning that over the next few centuries builds up to form a new ice cap.'

'But if that happened the seismic forces would have been incredible,' exclaimed Mark.

'Absolutely,' agreed Kei. 'It would have set off dormant volcanoes and caused huge earthquakes, creating massive tsunamis. So just imagine what would have happened to any civilizations? Cities and towns would have been destroyed, entire populations would have been wiped out, and any surviving social structures would have been totally undermined. Tidal waves would have destroyed anything that was within twenty miles of the coasts and icecaps thrust into warmer zones would have melted within a few years releasing huge volumes of water. Areas that were once fertile and densely populated would have been submerged. You know the old expression that civilization is just three meals away from savagery? Well most people would have been reduced to a new primitivism. Some survivors might not have been as badly affected as others, particularly those who lived in mountain regions, and they would have kept the some aspects of their culture alive. Parts of their towns and cities might have remained intact, for a while at least, and they would have retained knowledge of any technologies they might have had. The disaster that had befallen them would have been handed down as history that over time would have metomorphasized into legends and myth telling of a great flood that wiped out their civilization.'

'Its an interesting theory Kei,' said Mark. 'But I'm still not buying it, it doesn't really explain the structure we found in the desert. Surely if your theory is right it would also have been destroyed by the earthquakes which would have followed a slippage of the earth's crust or flooded by the deluge.'

'Maybe not. Suppose it was far enough inland to survive the tsunamis and subsequent rising sea levels and that it somehow withstood the earthquakes caused by shifting of the earth's crust. But its location in relation to the equator shifted drastically – tilting it away from its original alignment which would explain why that shaft was pointing north, rather than east towards the rising sun. Prior to the disaster it had been much further north in more temperate climate, similar to modern-day Europe, with fertile land allowing the people who had built it to survive, but with the displacement of the earth's crust it was hurled to a location much closer to the equator. The surrounding land would have quickly dried out and within a few hundred years become what is now the Sahara Desert and the structure would have been covered with sand, protecting it from the elements for thousands for years.'

22

LORCAN SAT AND STRUMMED A FEW notes on his
mandolin, which until quite recently had remained untouched for
more than 25 years. He played the main motif that made up the
tune Mactíre that he had recorded decades earlier and smiled as
he thought how such a simple arrangement of notes could have
brought about his meeting with his granddaughter. Irinda's mother
had contacted Lorcan through the record company which had
released the chart-topping dance single that had sampled his tune.
By that time he had retired from his job and using the royalties
from the record had bought the derelict house and plot of land
from Bridgeen Hanna where he lived as self-sufficiently as he could.
She wrote to tell him that her name was Kei and that she had been
married to Lorcan's son. Lorcan was initially stunned and suspected
that someone was trying to trick him and gain access to his new-
found modest wealth. Never-the-less he wrote back and said that
as far as he was aware he had no offspring but if any evidence to
the contrary was presented to him he would give it serious

consideration. The evidence was impressive and heartbreaking. It included a copy of a birth certificate for Wolfgang Mael Cliss O'Malley on which Lorcan was named as his father, with the word 'musiker' entered as his occupation, and Mandy Cliss as his mother. However, in an accompanying note Kei had told him that Mandy had died nearly 25 years earlier from cancer. The package she sent also included pictures of Wolf when he was growing up and Lorcan could not deny that they boy bore a striking resemblance to pictures of himself when he had been a child. There was also a picture of him as an adult with long tangled hair holding Irinda when she was a baby. Kei also sent the mandolin which he had abandoned, or rather forgotten when he had fled from Berlin. However, the clincher was a letter from Mandy which had never been sent. Kei attached a note explaining to Lorcan that Mandy had given it to her son before she had died as an introduction to his father if he ever decided to track him down.

It read: 'Lorcan. The last time we met you were on another planet. I can only assume you took something that, to use an old cliché, literally blew your mind. I hope you have been able to repair it. When I got back home that night I tried to tell you that I was pregnant. I had only found out earlier that day and had planned to wait a few weeks just to be sure before telling you. But when I saw you I knew that you needed something to shock you back into reality but you were far far away and I could only see terror in your eyes. I don't think my words ever penetrated the shell that you were building around you. I contacted your friend Eoghan and he came to Berlin and helped me to get you home, despite me keeping your passport. I think he told your embassy that you had lost it. I told Wolfgang all about you but when he was growing up I don't think he really understood why you were not with us. He is 17 now and maybe now that he is an adult he will accept that you were not well. I have asked him to contact you some day. I gave him your parent's address and other information that I had about you so I'm sure he will do so. In fact if you are reading this then he must have found you. All my love. Mandy.'

Lorcan was devastated when he read the letter and thought of all the lonely years he had spent trying to patch up his mind while Mandy was forced to bring up their child by herself. He imagined a life that they could have lived together if the drugs he had taken had not lacerated his sanity.

He immediately rang the phone number that Kei had sent to him in her letter and she told him that she would come to Ireland.

'Will my son be coming with you?' asked Lorcan excitedly.

'We are separated and he doesn't know that I have contacted you,' Kei replied. 'I haven't spoken to him in the last few months. He gets very caught up in his work.'

'That's a shame. It is a pity that he didn't stay with you. He must have known how difficult it was for his mother to bring up a child by herself.'

'Its OK, our decision to separate was mutual and he is in regular contact with Irinda. I have told her that she would soon get to meet you and she is quite excited.'

Lorcan was cautious.

'Her father has never tried to contact me. Will he not be annoyed that you have done so without telling him?'

Kei was silent at the other end of the phone for a few seconds.

'Maybe, but we agreed a long time ago that if one or other of us thought that something was for the best for Irinda then we should do it and I think it is important that she meets you. Wolf will just have to deal with that.'

'Wolf?' asked Lorcan startled.

'That is how he is known ... short for Wolfgang,' said Kei.

'Yes of course but it is such a strange coincidence.'

'How?'

'The tune I wrote, the famous one, is called 'Mactíre', which is the Irish for Wolf … it literally means son of the earth.'

Kei laughed.

'Oh he will love that. Hopefully me and Irinda will be able to persuade him to meet you. But we will come over first and see how we all get on.'

Lorcan drove to Shannon Airport to meet the flight from London carrying Kei and Irinda. He had printed their names on a sheet of paper and held it up as the passengers started to come through, scanning everyone to see if he could spot them. Kei had sent him a picture of Irinda when she was a baby sleeping in Wolf's arms but he was sure he would not be able to recognize her from this. The crowd had started to thin out when a Japanese woman dressed in jeans and a sweatshirt with a rucksack on her back came forward with a girl holding her hand.

'You must be Lorcan,' she said.

Irinda hid shyly behind her mother's legs, glancing occasionally at the wild-haired man who stood in front of them but turning away every time he looked back at her. Lorcan was stunned. He had not associated the foreign mispronunciation of English syllables he had heard in Kei's voice while talking with her over the phone with Japan and had thought she was, like his son, German. He tried to catch a glimpse of Irinda to see what she looked like.

'You will think me very old fashioned, but I don't think I have ever really met a Japanese person before, only seen them from afar jumping off a bus to take pictures before jumping on again and driving off,' he said to Kei by way of explanation.

'Does it matter?' asked Kei warily.

'No, God no, not at all,' blustered Lorcan. 'My God that must have sounded awful. You have to understand I've lived most of my life as a recluse and I still find it difficult to have conversations with Irish people and know what to say.'

Kei smiled at him reassuringly.

'Its traditional these days to embrace your daughter-in-law, even if they are separated from your son.'

'A son I have never seen.'

'There are no real rules in such a situation I suppose. But you can still give me a hug.'

'Delighted to,' said Lorcan, warming to Kei and noticing that Irinda emerged from behind her mother to watch as they embraced.

He hunched down beside her.

'Hello Irinda,' he said.

'Hi granda,' she said shyly, offering her hand for him to shake.

Kei was bemused by Lorcan's spartan cottage and Irinda was totally overwhelmed with excitement. They quickly made themselves at home and Lorcan could not even bear to think that they would only be staying for a short time. When Irinda went to bed that night Lorcan and Kei sat down and although Lorcan was still not sure of his ground with Kei he launched straight in to what was on his mind.

'Your husband has never got in touch and I didn't even know that he existed until you contacted me,' he said.

'Wolf didn't really talk much about you when we were together,' replied Kei.

'He mustn't have a very high opinion of me and I suppose I can't really blame him for that. He probably thinks that I simply abandoned his mother.'

'I believe he did think that for a long time but maybe in recent years he accepted that there must have been something badly wrong for you simply to disappear out of his and Mandy's life.'

'Did you ever meet Mandy?' asked Lorcan.

Kei shook her head.

'She died before I met Wolf but I think she is what inspired him to do what he does. Maybe too much?'

'How?'

'Wolf the ecowarrior is like a fiction. It is a character that he has invented and his true self has been sacrificed to allow this persona to live. He genuinely believes in what he is doing but his true nature is not the brash posturing action figure that he likes to portray.'

Lorcan nodded.

'So how did you manage to track me down?' asked Lorcan.

'I've had all the information for some time but I only started to go through it when I heard the tune you wrote. It was a big hit in Japan and when I saw a picture of you something seemed to click and I made the connection.'

'You were able to recognise me as Wolf's father from a picture?' said a startled Lorcan. 'I don't really see that much of a resemblance.'

Kei smiled and shook her head.

'I recognised you from when I saw you before,' she said.

Lorcan furrowed his brow in confusion.

'When was that?' he asked.

'Ten years ago when I was on a cycling holiday with Wolf. He insisted we take a detour down some bumpy mountain track and camp outside a house in the middle of nowhere. We knocked on the door of the house to ask directions and it was you who answered.'

Lorcan frowned trying to remember meeting Kei and his son but shook his head.

'I didn't really get many visitors and those who did call, like you, or rather like you pretended to be, were usually lost and looking for directions. I didn't pay too much attention. My goodness so you mean Wolf actually came to see me?'

'I couldn't put my finger on it at the time but I knew he was there for some reason for going off into the wilds like that,' said Kei. 'I also think that was the night that Irinda was conceived but I don't think that bit was planned.'

'But why did he not tell me who he was or try to contact me after that?' demanded Lorcan.

'I think it was something he often thought about. Five or six years ago Wolf took part in a campaign to stop a nuclear test in the Pacific Ocean. I think he really believed that he might die because he gave me a big box of stuff which he said his mum had passed on to him and contained information about how to contact his father. Wolf said if anything happened to him to let you know and to tell you about Irinda.'

'I remember hearing about that on the radio,' said Lorcan. 'The boats sailed into the middle of the test zone and no-one knew if the French government would go ahead with the nuclear test or not. I never really paid much attention to what was going on in the outside world but I was on the edge of my seat for days thinking of those people … and you tell me one of them was Wolf?'

Kei nodded and bit her lip.

'In some ways I never really got Wolf you know,' she said. 'I think it was an awful time for him but I was blasé about it all and I thought that he and everyone else were over dramatising. I was in Japan at the time and my parents were horrified – my mother is from Nagasaki and her mother saw the effects of the atom bomb in 1945 – I was sure that the test would not take place but maybe I was a little bit in denial as well.'

'It must have had a horrendous psychological affect on Wolf going through that. Surely you must have noticed he was different when he got back?'

'I didn't notice anything. The first thing Wolf did when he got ashore was to start screwing one of his eco groupies … and that wasn't the first time. We split up after that.'

'But he didn't take back the box he gave you?'

'I sort of forgot about it and maybe he did too. The next few years were pretty bad between us and we only really talked about Irinda, discussing her education and arranging meetings between her and Wolf. I had gone to live in New York with my new partner and left the box with some of my own stuff in my parent's basement. I think Wolf asked where it was once but it was almost as if he was just checking that it was somewhere safe and not that he wanted to get it back.'

'And what was in the box – the letters from Mandy I suppose and my mandolin?'

'That's it. But there were also letters from someone called Eoghan to Mandy and then some dated after her death to Wolf, explaining where you were living and working and basically giving an update on your condition.'

'Eoghan! He never said.'

Kei smiled.

'It was through him that I got your new address and found out that you seemed to be … erm more engaged with the world,' she said. 'He was suspicious but I was able to tell him enough about Mandy and Wolf to convince him I was genuine and he was delighted when I told him about Irinda and said that I wanted her to meet you.'

'He knew all along about Wolf?' exclaimed Lorcan.

Kei shrugged.

'Well what would you have done if you had known earlier?' she said.

Lorcan blustered but he had to accept that the knowledge he'd had a son would not have changed anything and that he would have been no less able to deal with world.

Kei and Irinda stayed for a week before returning to London and later that year at Christmas, Lorcan made his way by boat and train to stay in the apartment that Kei had rented in the English capital. It was the first time he had left Ireland in more than forty years, however, his apprehension about travelling was more than offset by his excitement at the prospect of meeting his granddaughter and her mother again. A few months later, at Easter, Kei and Irinda came back to Ireland and it was then that Kei dropped for Lorcan a bombshell and asked him to look after Irinda for three or four weeks while she went to northern Africa to take part in an archaeological dig.

23

TWO DAYS AFTER WOLF WAS RELEASED on bail Sophie arrived from Amsterdam.

'I hardly recognised you. Your hair has started to grow back. I thought you had shaved it because you were going bald,' she said as she embraced Wolf.

Wolf shrugged.

'I just fancied an image change at the time. Did you bring the briefcase?'

Sophie reached into the suitcase she had brought with her and drew out a battered black attaché case that looked as if dated from the 1960s.

'You could have got me into a lot of trouble coming through airport security,' she said. 'I didn't know the combination to open it.'

'Anyone who wanted to get in could have done so quick enough and there are only a few documents ... but thanks for trusting me.'

Wolf rolled the combination lock and clicked open the briefcase and rummaged through a few envelopes before pulling out a passport.'

Sophie looked bemused.

'Surely you don't have a false passport,' she exclaimed mockingly.

'Nothing false about it. It is totally legitimate,' replied Wolf. He hesitated before passing it to her. Sophie picked up the passport and saw that it was Irish and the name on it was Mael O'Malley. On the photo page was a picture of Wolf with a close-cropped head of hair and a pair of glasses.

'Bollox,' she exclaimed. 'Where did you get this?'

'I've had it for a few years now but only used it a couple of time when I wanted to be anonymous.'

Sophie smiled.

'You sly old bastard. How did you manage that.'

'My father was an Irishman called O'Malley who fucked off back to Ireland before I was born, although God knows how he managed to get out of the country because he left his passport behind and my mother used it to register my birth. The full name on my birth certificate is Wolfgang Mael Cliss O'Malley, although I have no idea how my mother came up with name Mael.'

'I always thought that 'Wolf' was some absurd macho handle that you had somehow persuaded people to call you … you know echoes of the wild and an endangered species.'

'My mother called me Wolfgang after her father and her surname was Cliss. I was always known as Wolfgang Cliss when I was growing up and over the years amassed enough official documentation to ensure that when I got my first German passport when I was a teenager that was the name that appeared upon it. When countries like the US started to slap bans on me entering I thought it might be useful to have an alternative identity and simply went to Dublin and applied for an Irish passport using my entirely legitimate birth certificate and a copy of my father's passport. I said that my second Christian name, Mael, and the surname O'Malley was how I was normally know. Its all totally legal.'

'So are you going to do a flit?' demanded Sophie.

'They have taken my German passport and I could be tied up in legal battles here for months,' sighed Wolf. 'Given the public hostility towards me I don't think this is a good place for me to be. And lets face it if you read some of the media reports could you blame people? I am being portrayed as the bad guy. I'll give it a few days and see how things pan out but can you put something in place in case I need to move quickly?'

'Already done so,' smiled Sophie. 'Just needs a bit of fine tuning.'

For the next three mornings Wolf reported to the nearby police station as required by his bail and returned with Jelka to her villa. He went early to avoid running into anyone else, but by the fourth day he knew that word must have got out for as he stepped from Jelka's car he heard a roar of abuse from the small crowd who had gathered outside. Police were there to keep them back and when he was inside the station Wolf asked if there was another station he could report to.

'That's for the court to decide,' said the policeman who pushed an attendance form forward for Wolf to sign.

'Well can you guarantee my safety if there are more people here tomorrow?' asked Wolf.

The policeman looked outraged at the suggestion and blustered about Wolf insulting his integrity and that of his officers. 'I don't mean here at the police station,' insisted Wolf. 'But there is a danger that someone might follow me back to the villa, it wouldn't just be myself who could be hurt but the people who are looking after me.'

'You can have a cell back at the main police station if you want,' said the policeman smugly. 'We are simply trying to accommodate you and can guarantee your safety only when you come and go from here but we are not here to provide you with a 24-hour-a-day private security service.'

Wolf nodded and walked back to the car where he saw Jelka fidgeting nervously. Once again the small crowd was kept at bay but he could see one man writing down the car registration and another vehicle pulling out from a row of parked cars as they drove off.

'We're being followed,' said Wolf. 'Perhaps you should go in a different direction.'

Jelka was shaking.

'I'm sorry about this, it was probably not what you were expecting,' said Wolf. 'Turn down the next street without indicating and then speed to the end.'

Jelka did what she was told and by the time the other car had reacted they were already turning again. Jelka managed to lose sight of the car and then pulled into a private cul-de-sac from where they saw their pursuers racing past. Jelka smiled nervously as she drove back into the street and back the way they had come and then by a circuitous route to her villa.

'Jelka I am going to betray your confidence,' said Wolf when they were safely in the compound.

'How? she demanded, although Wolf could see a sense of relief as she guessed what he was about to say.

'I think I am going to do a runner and by tomorrow morning you can phone the police and tell them that I have absconded,' said Wolf.

'How are you going to manage that? Are you just going to walk out the front door.'

'No I'm going to steal your boat when you go shopping at lunchtime.'

'I wish I was more able for these high dramas,' sighed Jelka. 'I thought it would be quite romantic and exciting having a subversive staying, but that frightened me this morning.'

Wolf nodded.

'Me too,' he said. 'I don't think it would take too long for anyone who wanted to find me here to track me down. I think the police and your government want me back in the cell where they can keep an eye on me and tell the public that I have effectively been locked up.'

'The public opinion does seem to be changing though. Some of the security guards are starting to talk and explain what actually happened,' said Jelka.

'That will change the minds of some people but there are interested parties in your government and the media who will keep insisting that I am to blame.'

Jelka nodded sadly.

'OK. I'll make lunch and then go and do that shopping you were telling me about,' she said.

Wolf phoned Sophie. They had already planned how to get him away from the house and agreed a coded conversation to put the operation in place.

'I think I am going to have to go back inside. It's getting to dangerous,' he said when she answered.

'When do you think you are going to go?'

'Just after lunch. Jelka is going to take me.'

'Will you be OK.'

'I'll keep my head down in the car.'

'Would you not be better getting the police to come for you?' asked Sophie.

'I don't want to draw too much attention to Jelka … its possible that people may have already identified her, so the less publicity the better.'

'OK I'll see you at the police station.'

Wolf hung up and held his phone up in the air to look at it.

'Work that one out you bastards,' he mouthed to himself before removing his battery and starting to pack his laptop and a change of clothes into his rucksack.

Wolf embraced Jelka and thanked her as she drove off. From an upstairs window he watched the car emerge into the street and as agreed Jelka turned her head to peer into the back seat and seemed to say something. A car pulled from the side of the road where it had been parked in a line with other cars and went off in the same direction. Jelka and her husband kept a small boat moored at the back of their house by a pier on the banks of the river. Wolf had already placed his backpack beside the gate in the walls which surrounded the house and which led to the pier. He felt vulnerable and exposed as he stepped onto the floating platform which was in clear view of the opposite bank where there was a public footpath and a grassland which opened out into the countryside surrounding Ljubljana. He was conscious that there could be more than one watch being kept on him, either by the police or more sinister elements and could not resist the urge to stoop low as he moved along the platform, making him look more suspicious rather than someone who was simply going for a sail along the river.

Wolf hefted his bag into the boat and went back to fetch the oars which he had leant by the gate, untied the mooring ropes and stepped down in to the little wooden vessel. He rowed less than 100 meters and then pulled onto far bank where Sophie was waiting for him.

'Well?' she demanded as he handed her his backpack and stumbled clumsily onto the river bank, kicking the boat out into mid stream as he did so from where it drifted back the way it had come towards the city.

Wolf looked anxiously around himself, conscious at how clumsy and amateur his escape was.

'I don't know. Lets not hang about,' he said. Sophie had parked a car close to the path and they jumped in with Sophie taking the drivers seat and starting off.

'So do we head straight for Austria?' asked Wolf.

'Italy,' said Sophie shaking here head. 'An old friend of yours is moored at Trieste and waiting to whisk you away.'

'Who?'

'More of an it really. El Acorde Perdido, although I don't know if Cathy Ovenbeck was able to sail it herself but she said she would get someone who we could trust. She suggested that you sail to Mallorca and stay in an old farm house that she knows of. It should just take a couple of days to get there and you can lie low for a week or two.'

Wolf nodded and even though he got the impression that Sophie was not giving him the full details he decided he would wait until they had crossed the border before asking for more information. They skirted the city before coming to a motorway and heading towards Italy. Wolf kept glancing behind him, half expecting to see flashing police lights at any moment.

'Do you want me to drive?' he asked Sophie.

'No I'm fine. I didn't even know you had a driving license.'

'Well I can drive but it has been a while. Same for you I take it.'

'Give me my old bicycle any day.'

Wolf and Sophie had both undertaken a number of anti-surveillance courses and they started to pick out certain cars and keep them in view as Sophie slowed down and sped up along the motorway but no-one seemed to be trying to keep them in view.

'So what's the plan then?' he asked as he saw a sign telling them that the border was just a few kilometres away.

'No plan. We just go for it,' said Sophie.

'Its just too bloody amateurish,' sighed Wolf, smiling as he remembered his stooping gait as he carried his stuff to the boat.

'Best way to be. Do you really want to be a professional fugitive?'

'Its not really a matter of choice.'

'Oh who's becoming a put-upon victim.'

Wolf and Sophie continued to banter and tease each other as came in view of a border post where a couple of guards lounged on chairs beside it. They glanced up casually as the car slowed and even nodded in return to Sophie's friendly wave. Another few metres and they saw a sign welcoming them to Italy and both simultaneously exploded into laughter.

Within half an hour they were driving down a steep winding road into Trieste and then following signs to the port. Sophie parked the car close to marina and they walked towards one of the promenades which jutted out into the Adriatic.

'So where is the boat and who is sailing it?' asked Wolf.

'Didn't I tell you?' said Sophie sheepishly and quickening her pace.

'Who are we meeting?' demanded Wolf.

'Over there,' nodded Sophie towards little boat that seemed like a toy beside the brash, ostentatious vessels beside it whose sole purposes in the world were to scream out how wealthy their owners were. The battered El Acorde Perdido nestled low in the water as if it was trying to be as inconspicuous as possible although it had in fact probably notched up more knots than all the other vessels that were moored nearby put together. The crew on a squat ugly yacht smiled patronisingly at Wolf and Sophie as they passed by. As Wolf threw his backpack on board the patched-up vessel he spotted Imma Mateus, grease-smeared and flustered, banging a spanner off the boat's tiny engine. She looked up and half-smiled and half-grimaced as Wolf and Sophie came on board.

'I think her best days are gone you know,' she said sighing sadly. 'A bit like yourself Wolf. How the hell did you end up in this little mess?'

'Its Mael now,' said Sophie hugging Imma.

Wolf embraced his former lover but he could feel her shoulders tensing at his touch. They had not met since the anti-nuclear campaign six years earlier in the Pacific Ocean and their second brief and intense relationship which had again ended acrimoniously and also sealed the end of Wolf's marriage to Kei.'

'Thanks for coming at such short notice,' said Sophie smiling brightly. 'Did you have a good journey?'

'I came from Mallorca … the trip was fine, but without a crew I didn't get any sleep,' said Imma.

'It won't take Wolf long to get his sea legs back and I'm sure he can do all the hard work on the journey back.'

'Hah … Mr Ecopunks is great at falling out of boats and getting his picture taken but I wouldn't trust him to scrub the decks. Are you not coming with us Sophie. Its been such a long time since we met?'

'I have abandoned my children with Niels's mother in Amsterdam. She thinks I am a loose woman anyway since I left her son and so I don't want her to have too much time to poison their minds. I think I can get a train to Vienna at 9.15 this evening and then I can travel on from there.'

Wolf nodded as if he was aware of this piece of information and tried to keep the sense of horror that he would be confined alone to the small boat for at least the next two or three days with Imma from gaining expression on his face.

'I don't think you should hang around,' said Sophie. 'It will not take the Llubljana authorities too long to realise that Wolf has gone underground and you should maybe put a few miles between yourselves and the Slovenian coast before the word gets out. Beside you are not exactly the most inconspicuous vessel and crew in town.'

'The engine is about to pack up so we will have to depend on wind power all the way,' sighed Imma.

'Where are we going?' asked Wolf.

'Back to Mallorca. I have a house there – or at least my parents do. Don't worry they're not there.'

'Fine,' said Wolf trying to smile and ignore the barely suppressed smirk on Sophie's face.

'Great,' she said. 'So Wolf lie low there for a few weeks, grow your hair and beard a bit longer, keep those glasses on, get a suntan and become Mr O'Malley.'

'O'Malley,' laughed Imma. 'Don't tell me you going to pretend to be Irish?'

'Oh you two have so much catching up to do,' said Sophie. 'I better go. Take care and get in touch soon.'

Wolf and Imma both embraced Sophie before Imma unmoored the boat and started the smoking engine to propel them away from their dock and into the open sea before cutting it and raising a sail.

24

DURING THE VOYAGE TO MALLORCA FROM Trieste someone had to be constantly awake to steer the boat and trim the sails when necessary. Wolf knew the bare basics of sailing and so Imma only left him alone when she felt the simplest manoeuvres would need to be carried out. She would sleep for just a couple of hours at a time and come on deck to check all was well. To start with their conversations were restricted to a few inanities but soon they began to relax into each other's company and they were even able to laugh at their previous flings.

They docked at a little harbour in a town called Porto Cristo on the east coast of Mallorca where Imma had left her car and she drove the short distance to her finca which was set on the side of a dusty red hill surrounded by olive trees and with a view over to a crumbling monastery on to of a scar of rock and in the distance the shimmering sea. Imma left Wolf to explore the house and surrounding grounds while she drove off again to get a few supplies. When she arrived back she had a newspaper in which she showed a picture of Wolf in his dreadlocked days and a smaller more recent one with his head shaved.

'Your still making the headlines,' she said patting the now thickly growing stubble on his head.

Wolf looked at the news report and could just about get the gist of what it said. Imma translated the passages he had difficulty with. The report basically covered speculation about how he had managed to escape Slovenian justice and where he was now.

'And where am I?' he asked.

Imma squinted back at the paper as she cut up peppers and courgettes for their evening meal.

'Austria or Germany seems to be the main consensus,' she said. 'No mention of Italy or anywhere else.'

'What was the Slovenians' reaction?'

'They seem to be just blustering about the need for justice to carried out, although there seems to be one or two dissenting voices suggesting that there was no real reason to keep you in custody. I wouldn't get too relaxed though because a government minister is insisting that if you turn up in an EU country you should be immediately arrested and send back.'

Imma started cooking while Wolf went off to shower and change. Imma did the same before they ate and afterwards they sat side by side on a sagging sofa.

'I take it you are no longer with Kei?' Imma asked him.

Wolf shook his head.

'We keep in touch fairly regularly but that is usually to discuss Irinda and arrange times that I can spend with her. They seemed to be fairly settled in Japan but moved to London last year, although I haven't seen them since the summer. I want to take a bit of time out soon and catch up with Irinda before she forgets who I am.'

'Did you never meet anyone else, long-term I mean?'

178

'Well no. Three or four-month things but they never seemed to go anywhere and I often got the feeling that they were with me out of curiosity rather than because I am a fun and loving person to be with.'

Imma nodded thoughtfully.

'You were never that.'

'What about you?' asked Wolf.

'I broke up with my partner last year. We'd been together for five or six years but I guess it was time to move on. That's why I moved to Mallorca, just to get away from everything for a bit,' she said.

Wolf was surprised at how easily he began a new affair with Imma although she seemed quite blasé about at all, as if there was nothing more natural in the world. The finca was in the hills to the east of the island, well away from the tourist resorts. The house itself was a large stone building, sparsely furnished and decorated, its whitewashed walls providing cool relief from the Mallorcan sun and the air inside always seemed to have the faint whiff of smoked wood. The surrounding grounds were poorly tended, the dry red soil providing little sustenance for anything but the hardiest plant life. The days were long and lazy and Wolf and Imma often lay in bed until late. They went walking together in nearby hills and Imma taught Wolf a few Mallorquian phrases and recipes. Occasionally they drove to some obscure location on the coast which compared to those in the resorts that they had driven through were empty and those who were there managed to space themselves far enough apart to give each other their privacy.

Wolf also found time for more solitary explorations. He found a rusted moped in a shed beside the finca and after a morning working at the machine and cleaning down its moving parts he was able to start it. The nearest large town to the finca was Manacor and Wolf rode there on several occasions. The town's ugly industrial exterior hid a web of narrow, shadowed streets where green and brown shuttered buildings on either side echoed the farting Vespa engine. He parked the bike to meander on foot and assimilate the town's strangeness – there was nothing spectacular about Manacor but something about it intrigued him. He imagined himself living anonymously in these streets and creating a private sanctuary behind one of these shuttered windows.

On another occasion he drove out of the town and towards the coast, cutting off from the main road onto a dirt track where he found a whole network of little laneways cutting through the Mallorcan countryside. The landscape was one of barren fields and sun-wasted shrubs clinging to life in the poor rocky soil. The tracks ran close to the coast of high rocky cliffs and narrow little coves. Dust scooted from beneath the wheels of the moped as it hopped from dip to hollow. Wolf slowed to a halt and gazed into a steep inaccessible cove where the water lay blue and clear. He cut the engine and flopped onto the dry grass to listen to the sound of chirping insects and the bubble and slap of the sea below him.

He relished the anonymity of life on the island and felt for the first time in years that he was able to be himself rather than the invented persona that he had become. Even during the time he had spent meditating in the ashram in India he had never really been able to shake of the myth that he was living and in fact had spend most of his time inventing the new bald-headed ecowarrior persona that he had been living for the past few years.

He was not sure how he would deal with being Mael O'Malley rather than Wolf Cliss. It would undoubtedly bring its own problems not least in terms of how he would make a living. For most of his life he had lived a hand-to-mouth existence, living off state benefits and the goodwill of fellow campaigners who fed him and gave him shelter. However, following the AKNR experience Wolf knew that he was being watched and that there were those who would use the information they had gathered on him to pounce on the least misdemeanour. He was determined to live as openly and honestly as he could. After the ecopunks website was relaunched Niels took a decision to run it as a commercial operation. He was very selective in the adverts he accepted for the site and also set up an online store selling tee-shirts, posters, CD and books as well more practical items such as rucksacks and hammocks. The site was soon generating enough income to pay Niels, Sophie and Wolf a modest salary as well as other regular contributors. Inevitably some elements had alleged that they were now using the cause of the environment to feather their own nests but some of those elements would have also pointed the finger of accusation at them if they had continued to claim benefits while more or less working full time on the website.

Now that he was no longer Wolf the ecowarrior, Wolf felt he had no right to continue as editor of the site. His right to that post and the validity of his opinions had been earned through his campaigning credentials. Mael O'Malley was no-one as far environmental campaigners were concerned, besides which Wolf did not want to make it easy for anyone to make the link between the two names. He did not doubt that someone would do so before long and that his new identity would be revealed but he was prepared for that. It might generate comment and publicity but he was sure people would quickly forget and prefer to remember the mythical Wolf.

As well as earning an income there were other issues he had to consider. The persona of Wolf had ensured that when he had wanted to travel anywhere in the world he could get a free lift, usually on the ship, or sometimes chartered train, of one of the larger environmental campaign groups. Other wealthy supporters would put their yachts at his disposal. Wolf always made sure that there was some valid reason for these journeys either getting him to where some campaign was taking place or to lend his support to a group who were looking publicity for their causes. However, it also enabled him to visit Irinda when she had lived in Japan or at least somewhere close to her home without her having to fly to Europe. He hoped that Kei would understand his new circumstances if she chose to move back there, although he wondered what her reaction would be when she discovered that he was living, at least temporarily, with Imma. Other perks of his previous lifestyle would also be lost to him now but in the balance he felt that no longer having to be Wolf Cliss outweighed those.

He was tired when he got back to the finca but decided that he should check his emails – something he had been avoiding since he had arrived there as he knew it would thrust him back into being Wolf, for a while at least. He opened up his laptop and plugged it into a phone socket and waited for an internet connection. There were more than a hundred new emails which, judging from the subject lines, were mostly messages of support from friends and other activists. However, one made him suddenly stop scrolling and click it open.

Wolf had been hoping that a message from his daughter would catch his eye but the sight of Kei's name and the word urgent typed in the subject line had caused him a flash of anxiety.

Kei must have anticipated this because the first sentence read 'Irinda and I are both well'. However, what followed was of little comfort to Wolf and set him scowling.

'I think Marco is in trouble. He emailed me and asked if you would help. I tried to call him but got no response. I am genuinely worried and wouldn't ask you to follow up if I didn't think it was serious. I and Irinda are spending a bit of time in Ireland, I thought she should know about that part of her heritage as well. Can you call me or her when you get a chance? Kei.'

Wolf was as much taken aback to find that his daughter and ex-wife were in Ireland as he was to learn that Marco had asked for his help.

25

AFTER THE EXCITEMENT OF THE FIRST morning that Kei returned from Africa and Irinda was assured that she was not leaving again and that her father was safe, Kei told Lorcan about the message she had received from her former partner.

'What sort of trouble is he in?' asked Lorcan.

'He didn't say but it must be bad if he asked Wolf to meet him.'

'But if Wolf is effectively on the run is it not possible that your friend Marco is trying to flush him out?' asked Lorcan cautiously, conscious that he was treading on delicate territory.'

Kei nodded.

'I don't think Marco would try to track him down through me if that was the case,' she said. 'Of course, I could be wrong and there is a danger that his employers, or one of the governments with who they work are using Marco to find Wolf. But he will be aware of that and I'm sure he will take precautions. I got an email from Sophie, who is one of his closest friends, and she told me that he is no longer in Slovenia and left the country using an alias, although she didn't tell me where or what name he was using.'

'Its all very cloak and dagger. I hope he is OK, I would actually like to meet him some day,' said Lorcan.

'I haven't told him that we are with you but I think he will work it out for himself.'

Later that evening Kei began to tell Lorcan about the dig she had been working on and its inconsistency with current theories about the origins of human civilizations.

'It's bigger than Newgrange – the passage is wider and the chambers inside are much larger,' she said. 'In Newgrange the central chamber is only a few metres long but the main chamber in the Saharan structure is three or four times that size and three ante-chambers lead off from it as opposed to the alcoves that you find at Newgrange. It is almost as if the Irish site is a scale model of the much bigger structure in Africa – a representation rather than a complete replica.'

Lorcan nodded.

'And what about the carvings? Are there any similarities with those you would find in passage tombs and standing stones in Ireland?' he asked.

'None at all,' said Kei. 'The ones in the desert are much … I don't know … denser, I suppose, more intricate and they can be found on every surface. Even the floor. Also there are regular alcoves with bowls carved into the rock and clear evidence of scorching. Mark and I both agreed that fires must have been lit there to light the passage and the central chambers.'

'But your colleague Mark does not believe that is 12,000 years old?' said Lorcan.

'Can't believe it, is more like it,' sighed Kei. 'And who can blame him. It flies in the face of so much archaeological data. There has been a lot of speculation about ancient human civilizations predating those which are known to conventional historians but there is not really that much hard evidence, it is often based on conjecture. Those who speculate on such civilizations are ridiculed by mainstream archaeologists and Mark is strictly mainstream.'

'So how does he account for the structure in the desert?' asked Lorcan.

'He thinks that a wandering tribe linked to the passage grave and tomb builders who lived in Europe around 2000BC must have settled there and built it.'

'But surely he accepts that that region of North Africa was desert at that time.'

'He just keeps coming up with excuses, such as that it must have been an oasis that subsequently dried out and the structure was covered by sand.'

'What about the stone. How does he think it was transported there?'

'Slave labour. According to his theory the builders would have been the descendants of the original European tomb builders and their techniques would have been much more sophisticated than anything you would have here in Ireland or on the European continent. He argued that the builders of the African structure would have learned from their ancestors and improved upon their techniques and kept building and improving on the original prototypes.'

'But you think it is possible that it could be the other way round, with a decline in skills?'

'Yes. It strikes me that the European passage tombs such as those at Newgrange are modelled on the one that we found in the Sahara, an approximation of the original, built with a high degree of skill and knowledge of astronomical alignment, a remarkable feat given

186

the tools and materials that were available, but lacking the sophistication of the original.'

'You said one of the mummies you found in the Sahara seemed to be Caucasian with red hair?'

'I think this is where part of Mark's problem lies. A lot of the alternative history material does sound a bit like an Aryan master-race theory,' said Kei. 'Many of the legends they focus on tell of tall, white-skinned people with fair or red hair tramping the globe thousands of years ago and being treated as gods by primitives.'

Lorcan nodded thoughtfully.

'But the legends do not just focus on white people … I mean here in Ireland, among our early myths, we have a race of people known as a the Fomorians who were said to be dark skinned. Early Gaelic literature refers to them as 'Corca Oidce' – which means 'people of darkness' – or 'Hi Dorchaide' – 'sons of the dark'. They were said to be the original inhabitants of Ireland described as being giants who defeated all invaders until they were driven to the western islands by the Fir Bolgs and later the Tuatha de Dannan … who by a strange coincidence were said to be a tall, pale-skinned and golden-haired race of people. Another interesting fact is that the name Fomor may be derived from the Irish faoi-mhuir which means 'from beneath the sea' and which gives us the modern Irish word for submarine 'fomhuireán'.'

'That would tie in with the flood myths,' exclaimed Kei. 'The alternative historians argue that many of the world's most ancient monuments such as the Sphinx in Egypt, the temples at Angkor Wat in Cambodia and the ruined city at Tiahuanaco in the Bolivian Andes were influenced by a much more ancient culture which was all but wiped out by a global flood and which is commonly dated to around 10500BC,' she said.

'I see where you are coming from,' said Lorcan. 'Maybe the Formarians were African survivors of the deluge?'

'Maybe. There were also people known as the Olmec, who are believed to have been of African descent, who became a god-like race in Mexico.'

'I thought Quetzalcoatl was the major deity in Mexico?' said Lorcan.

'Yet another tall, white man – often depicted with a beard,' said Kei, rummaging through her books and print-outs. 'There is more known about him, or at least the legends that surrounded him, than the Olmec. Quetzalcoatl is also known as the 'plummed serpent'. According to a documents dating to the time of the Spanish Conquistadores, who arrived in modern-day Mexico in the 1500s, the Aztecs still revered Quetzalcoatl, building huge pyramids in his honour.'

Kei lifted one of her books and opened it at a marked page and began to read: 'One contemporary Spanish commentator said the Aztecs described him as 'a fair and ruddy-complexioned man with a long beard. He was a mysterious person, a white man with a strong body, broad forehead, large eyes and a flowing beard. He came from across the sea in a boat that moved by itself without paddles. He condemned sacrifices, except of fruits and flowers and was known as the god of peace'.'

'I though the Aztecs were notorious for carrying out human sacrifices and slaughtered thousands of people at a time by slicing them open a ripping out their still beating hearts,' said Lorcan.

'You're right. But then they wouldn't be the first people to distort what was essentially a message of love to justify horrendous violence – just look at some of your peace-loving Christains' said Kei.

'The description of Quetzalcoatl is very similar to the Tuatha de Dannan,' said Lorcan. 'They were said to have come to Ireland from the sky, although other reports said that they came by sea and then set fire to their vessels so that it seemed that they appeared to come from a cloud. They were described as being tall and fair and descended from the goddess Danu. They were great warriors, fine poets, wise in the ways of nature and medicine and said to possess magical skills. One of their kings was called Nuada who lost a hand in battle. However, a physician called Diancecht made him an artificial hand from silver ... other stories tell how Nuada's original hand was restored by surgery.'

Lorcan leafed through the internet printouts and books that Kei had given him and asked her to play the film footage again of the structure she had been excavating in the Sahara.

'That doesn't really do it any justice,' she said. 'The way the light seemed to flicker in there made those carvings seem to dance as if they were constantly shape shifting.'

'I wish I could have seen it ... but you do get a sense of that from your film,' said Lorcan.

He smiled sheepishly. 'This may sound absurdly pretentious but after I took the LSD my mind moved beyond purely conscious perceptions into areas that are normally only accessed by the unconscious and which are often kept pretty obscure because we are asleep and dreaming and usually only have a vague concept of what we dreamt about,' said Lorcan.

Kei frowned, unsure where Lorcan's discourse was going or even what had prompted it.

'Such as?' she said uncertainly.

'Well in dreams we can fly, talk to dead people and move from one scenario to another without any sense of physical displacement.'

'Ok go on.'

'But during that LSD trip that area of my psyche which I had

189

previously only been vaguely aware of while dreaming was shown to my fully-conscious mind and the fog between the two realities was lifted. I could see the universe in its fullness and vastness and my mind couldn't cope ... it shredded trying to assimilate what was being shown to it. It was like a power surge that blew fuses all over the place and which I have never been able to fully repair, although I think I have been able to patch up the circuitry to a point where I am able to function like something resembling a human being, although a somewhat erratic one.'

'Sounds nightmarish,' said Kei.

'It was ... still is sometimes but I can control it to an extent now.'

'How?'

'Well to illustrate what I mean, there was an English poet called Robert Graves, who was also a mythographer and who wrote historic novels. He was badly wounded during the First World War and suffered from shell shock for the rest of his life. It was a different trigger but similar in a way I think to what happened to my mind after I took the LSD. Anyway he used to claim that he was able to gain unique insights into his subject matter through what he called analyptic analysis.'

'I don't understand,' sighed Kei.

'He would totally immerse himself in his subject and sink into a sort of trance and let the images that emerged become part of the historical truth of whatever subject he was researching.'

'Sounds a bit suspect ... I mean it could be just a shortcut for doing proper research and backing up your own preconceptions.'

'It is definitely fraught with dangers and should only be used sparingly and when all other source materials have been exhausted,' agreed Lorcan shuffling the papers. 'But this subject here – the hypothesis that an ancient human civilization was destroyed by some global catastrophe is quite sparse on raw material ... we have a lot of speculation going on, based on some very vague facts. If ever a subject deserved a bit of fleshing out it is this one.'

'How do you propose to do that?' said Kei, unable to avoid letting a note of scepticism enter her voice.

'Well I have already been using the analyptic technique to research the life of Mael Mac Datho for a biography I have been working on.'

'Mael, that's one of Wolf's aliases,' said Kei. 'Mael O'Malley, believe it or not.'

Lorcan smiled sadly.

'Mandy must have told him of my interest. Even in those days I was always talking about him.'

'So who was Mael Mac Datho?'

'He was an 11th century Irish monk and a bard. We have fragments of his verse surviving in all sorts of formats and various references to him. Several ballads that are still sung are based on his poems. He is believed to have been ordained in a monastery in Co Down, close to the Mourne Mountains, where my father's family originally came from. But there are references and folklore relating to Mac Datho in religious communities and even secular settlements in other parts of the country. He is said to have travelled in Europe and to the Holy Lands in his time and there is whiff of scandal about him … liaisons with women and maybe even a couple of illegitimate children. Some of this can be found in written accounts dating from the time but most of it was gathered in later centuries by folklorists. Even the verses that survive and that are attributed to him are for the most part transcriptions from oral renderings made five or six centuries after Mac Datho died. What I have done is gather as much of this material as possible and, using Graves analyptic method, tried to get inside of Mael Mac Datho's mind and to almost become him.'

'Have you succeeded?' asked a bemused Kei.

'Well as you have stated it is not an exact science, but I think I have been able to construct a life story that holds together in terms of chronology and motives and to maybe reconstruct more accurate versions of Mac Datho's poems than the existing ones, many of which have become corrupted through oral transmission over many years. This entailed learning old and middle Irish and spending several years schooling myself in complex bardic metres and rhyming schemes.'

Kei looked alarmed.

'I don't know if we'll be around for several years Lorcan. We'll come back and visit, but … ' she said.

'No, God I don't mean that but what I am saying is that I could at least use those techniques and see what comes up. The material we have is scant but I'm sure I could open my mind to it … this astronomic alignment that keeps cropping up and the various flood myths. Give me a day or two to read up on it and let it all sink in to this slightly fused old computer in my head and we'll see what emerges.'

'Why not,' said Kei. 'It can't do any harm.'

26

WOLF, EDGY AFTER A FORTY-MINUTE flight, caught the Metro from the airport into the centre of Madrid and made his way by a circuitous route to Ramon's suburban apartment. Ramon was a former soldier who had worked for his country's intelligence services before retiring and setting up a counter-surveillance training business. He had no particular interest in environmental issues but Wolf had attended a series of courses he had run in Holland. Despite a huge difference in their political outlook – which became apparent after Ramon brusquely turned down Wolf's suggestion that if Ramon provided the classes free it would be in the broader interest of the environment – they had got on well together. Wolf decided to continue attending the course, on a purely business agreement by paying for Ramon's services and knowledge.

'I'm glad to see someone who may actually put my teaching into practice rather than the usual macho young businessmen who like to give themselves a sense of self importance by believing that they could be the victims of industrial espionage,' Ramon had told Wolf.

After the course they had kept in touch and Ramon had often invited Wolf to visit if he was ever in Madrid. Now that he was about to take up that offer Wolf was aware that he was taking a risk by going to him because he could not be sure that Ramon would not shop him to the Spanish police as a fugitive from Slovenian justice as soon as he rang his doorbell. Ramon answered the door himself and greeted Wolf with a bear hug before ushering him in and introducing him to his wife who looked frail and pale compared to her burly and tanned husband.

'This is my fugitive friend,' he said to his wife, who simply smiled and asked Wolf what he wanted to drink.

'You've been watching the news then,' said Wolf, still trying to test his ground.

Ramon shrugged casually.

'That is your business … although I think as your tutor I am entitled to know how you managed to get out Slovenia.'

'A ship in the night,' replied Wolf, warming quickly again to Ramon, despite his worries.

'Yes but you arrived here by air … you must have had some ID. Surely you are not so clumsy to be travelling on false papers … you're too well known for that?'

'My papers are entirely genuine and I am entirely legitimate and despite their protestations the Slovenians have not yet asked for an international warrant for my arrest,' said Wolf.

'Good but I hope you are still taking precautions,' said Ramon.

Wolf nodded smugly.

'I took the metro from the airport, caught a taxi to an address in the suburbs that I picked at random from a phone book, walked for a bit, then caught a bus back into the city, stopped for a coffee and had a good look around me, two more metros and another coffee, checking constantly for any sign of surveillance, before I got a taxi here,' he said. 'But as you constantly reminded us, if someone really wants to get me and has the resources to put a whole team on my trail they we can expect a knock on the door very soon, otherwise I should be fine.'

Ramon nodded.

'Mobile phone,' he demanded. Wolf took his phone from his pocket and handed it over to Ramon, who shook it.

'Good. You've taken the battery out,' he said. 'Although I still maintain that you are better without these things at all. To me they are just a self-planted tracking device and those dickhead young entrepreneurs who keep me in this luxurious semi-retirement always seem determined to have the latest model.'

'You are sounding more paranoid than I am,' said Wolf.

'No that is not possible because I don't need to hide from anyone, well at least not anymore,' replied Ramon. 'And the truth is that neither do most other people who come to me ... present company excluded of course.'

'So you are still deluding yourself that all is well with the world ... democracy is at work in Spain and the European Union and that private law-abiding citizens have nothing to fear.'

A smile spread over Ramon's face as he remembered how well Wolf could goad him into a debate.

'Just because you are on the run doesn't mean that the rest of society has to be looking over its shoulder,' he said. 'Why are you so paranoid on the rest of our behalf?'

Wolf nodded over to a television that sat in a corner on which a game show was being played out. He could hear the sound of another television in the kitchen where Ramon's wife was clattering around and preparing supper.

'Karl Marx described religion as the opium of the people but in modern times that could be substituted by television,' he said. 'It keeps people sedated and prevents them from asking too many questions. Who cares about CO_2 emissions or wars in obscure parts of Africa or the Middle East when you can numb your mind by tuning into the latest love triangle or dramatic plot twist on some soap opera or follow the fortunes of a third-rate group of singers trying to win what was once known as a talent competition. Religion once offered you the hope of eternal salvation, although that was a long-term bet, but TV can bring you instant gratification, an easy way to forget the harsh realities of everyday life and lose yourself in someone else's dramas. It even offers the hope of salvation through reality programmes where previous non-entities can suddenly be plucked from obscurity and plunged without any effort into a world of celebrity paradise and financial success. While with religion people used to look to saints and martyrs as an example of how they could achieve grace and salvation it is now the latest reality TV star. Someone who just a few days ago was caught in the same drudgery as most ordinary people now has, by the power of TV, been transformed and taken to a paradise on earth. They might be dumped back into reality a few months later but by then the viewers will have found someone else to pin their hopes on.'

'You make it all sound as if it was some sinister government plot to keep people in their places,' said Ramon.

'If that is case then those governments must be rubbing their hands with delight because it is a pretty convenient way of keeping the spotlight off them and even if it isn't a conspiracy theory, which I admit it probably isn't, it is all very convenient. Newspapers and magazines have almost become part of the entertainment industry whereby their lead stories are often about the sexual peccadilloes of some football star or the drugs problem of a teenage pop singer.

Crime is also big news – a brutal murder or rape gets huge coverage followed by anguished editorials on the need for a clampdown on law and order and demands that the government does more which of course they promised they will do. But all that helps to take attention away from the everyday reality that the so-called freedoms of the western world are fairly shallow ones. Some people catch on and ask questions but they are too few to upset the balance and they are generally regarded as cranks and if they are too vociferous they are described as radicals, giving them a slightly sinister veneer.'

'Are you talking about yourself?' asked Ramon.

'Too an extent yes. I had become a cliché and so I shaved off my dreadlocks and abandoned my habitual combat gear in favour of a more sober image. I was consciously trying to play the game and create a new media profile for myself and my new appearance had the effect of transforming me into an almost respectable 'green philosopher' although many media outlets still preferred to refer to me as an 'ecoterrorist'. I wanted try to move away from the more maverick style of campaigning which I was used to and to become more issue focused. That's why I spent more time working on the ecopunks website. I believed I had established my credentials with the hard-core activists, by getting my hands dirty and being involved in grass roots campaign, I had a high profile outside those who normally take an interest in environmental issues. I hoped to make our campaigns more mainstream and give the issues a broader acceptance. Except of course it backfired on me.'

'How?'

'People lost interest in what I was doing – they liked the wacky hippy who was always getting arrested. We live in a throwaway culture where the three-minute news package or dramatic pictures and dramatic headlines informs our lives. The big gesture makes the news, considered debate and informative articles are not sexy.'

'But are you not being overly critical of television?' asked Ramon. 'At its best it can be informative and educational and at its worst mind-numbingly boring and tedious, but then sometimes people need that just to wind down.'

'Fair enough, some people drink, some take drugs and some dull their minds and try to relax and unwind with television, some do all three at the same time ... and I suppose that is all very well if it is done in moderation. But if someone was taking too much drink you would be concerned that they are damaging their health and tell them to stop. Yet for some people that is what is happening with TV. It is switched on in the morning – perhaps has been on from the night before – and stays on and people watch it for the sake of watching it, not because they find what is on particularly interesting or stimulating but because it is there and stops them from thinking. It acts as a sedative. Now 24-hour-a-day sedatives are not healthy ... and even ones which are taken for six of seven hours a day are not particularly healthy either.'

Wolf and Ramon passed the rest of the evening cajoling one another, debating and challenging each other's position. It was stimulating for Wolf for he was normally surrounded by people who shared his outlook on life and often hung on his every word as a philosophical pearl of green wisdom. Kei had been an exception, although she was not opposed to what Wolf believed, she could not accept it as a doctrine to live by. She very rarely made any demands off him and so the simple request to help Marco was something that he felt he could not ignore.

Using one of his proxy email addresses he had written from Mallorca to the Peruvian at the address, also an alias, which Kei had forwarded to him and almost immediately received a reply.

Marco wrote: 'I have some information which I want you to have.

I was involved in some research which even I found questionable and also obtained some data which my company are trying to suppress. Unfortunately I think they know that I have this material and given our mutual acquaintance they probably suspect that I am going to pass it on to you. Even without knowing it you have managed to fuck up life again. Thanks. Anyway, I will pass this on to you but it is quite technical and we need to meet so that I can explain it. This is not a trap. You can trust me. Ha ha ha! I am in Madrid. If you can meet me there please let me know and I will forward you an address.'

Wolf's inclination as not to answer, he was also worried about breaking cover so soon after his escape from Slovenia. Although he was now bearded and his hair had grown and he had his new identity it would not take too much work for someone who had the resources to identify him as the fugitive Wolf Cliss. The only thing that inclined him to reply was that it was Kei who had asked him to help. Imma had rolled her eyes when he gave her an outline of what was happening but she didn't object.

From Ramon's apartment he set out the next morning to find an internet cafe where, as previously agreed, he emailed Marco. Within a couple of minutes he received a reply with a contact phone number. Wolf left the internet cafe and found a public phone from where he rang the number.

'Hola, Wolf,' came the reply.

'Hi Marco. Are you OK?' replied Wolf.

'Shitting myself,' said Marco.

'Are you safe?'

'I think I am fine here but it is afterwards that I am worried about.'

'You don't have to go ahead,' said Wolf. 'I mean I'm not even sure that I will be able to do anything with this information that you say you have for me. I'm eh … not as involved with the ecopunks crowd any more.'

'I think you'll find it interesting for what it is and if you think it is appropriate you can maybe pass it on.'

'Fine. I'll be there in two hours. Where will I meet you?'

Marco gave him an address and they rang off. Wolf decided to put the training that Ramon had given him into use again and went to a cafe for half an hour to look around himself. He then began an elaborate journey on foot, by bus, taxi and metro that involved stopping at several more cafes and a trip to a supermarket before he arrived at metro station closest to the address Marco had given him.

He stepped from the stifling claustrophobia of the metro station into the glaring sun. The old streets of this part of the city seemed to confine and amplify the constant din of traffic and afternoon bustle. A blind man stood on a corner selling lottery tickets, slung in a necklace from his shoulders. Shop windows hung with meat, fruit and sweets lined the streets. All around him buildings crumbled, their pitted shells peeling to display crudely layered brick. His senses were prickling as Wolf took in the sights, sounds and smell of the street, fixing his eyes on passers-by, scanning faces and passing cars. He came to a gate set in a wall with a panel of buttons set beside and buzzed the apartment number which Marco had given him. A speaker crackled a monotoned, sexless reply and Wolf bent his head to the dull, grey grill and spoke his name. A buzzer sounded and a bolt clicked back. The gate swung open at a push from his hand and he stepped through to a shaded courtyard with a fountain splaying droplets on his head. Wolf crunched across the yard to a second panel of buttons but this time there was no reply, just a buzz and whirr of a lock. Inside an elevator carried him up to the fourth floor and to his left he saw a door standing ajar. Wolf knocked but there was no reply and so he pushed his way in.

Whoever had killed Marco had obviously done so with a level of commitment that suggested more than simply a desire to end a man's life. The Peruvian's feet and hands had been tied behind his back and a wire noose twisted into his neck, cutting deep into the flesh. Given the look fixed on Marco's face, Wolf presumed it had been a slow process. Whoever had done it had wanted Marco to suffer. Wolf tried to rationalise the bitterness he still felt towards Marco for the role he played in ending his relationship with Kei and the empathy he felt for the terror that the dying man must have felt. It was almost tangible.

He looked around the apartment and saw the mess in which he was standing had an unmistakable order to it. Drawers and cupboards had been emptied and their contents sifted before being pushed into the centres of the various rooms to make way for further searches. In one pile he could see Marco's Peruvian passport and a wallet with credit cards and cash. Other valuables, including a watch and a gold signet ring, nestled in the various piles. Wolf decided to get out of the flat quickly. It was clear that Marco had not buzzed him in and the killer must still nearby, either lying in wait for him or else he was being set up. What better stitch-up could there be than to ensure that a bitter cuckolded husband who was ideologically opposed to everything that his rival had stood for was found in the same room as a still-warm murder victim.

Wolf looked out through the shuttered windows into the noisy street but could see nothing abnormal. He went to the apartment door and out into the hallway where he wedged open the elevator door to make sure it couldn't be called and clocked a fire escape at the far end of the hallway. He cursed himself for going back into the apartment and leaving himself vulnerable in such a way.

'Sixty seconds,' he mumbled to himself and started counting down, losing his place at 53 as he heard the sound of a siren.

'Fuck,' he exclaimed but went back into the apartment and tried to let his frantic mind assimilate the murder scene.

Wolf knew that Marco was a computer nerd. All his information would have been stored on his laptop but although there was a desk in the sitting room and leads running from a printer and a phone point, there was no laptop. The killer must have taken that. However, Wolf was sure that if Marco had tried to alert him, via Kei, that he had information he wanted to give him that he would have taken steps to transfer it into a format in which he could pass on. Saving it onto a disc was obvious but given the way the apartment had been upturned Wolf assumed that Marco's killer had also been looking for the very same thing and may even have found it.

The sound of the police siren was getting closer and Wolf had counted down to twenty.

He looked at the printer and saw a light flashing and paper in the feeder. Pulling a tissue from his pocket to cover his thumb he hit the print button. Ten sheets of paper with closely typed data flew off the machine. Wolf grabbed them and bolted from the apartment and down the stairwell. As he left the apartment building he could hear the sound of the siren in the street out beyond the courtyard. Rather than going through the steel gateway through which he had entered he hurried to the side of the building hoping that he would find another exit. There was none and he stopped to consider his options. The wall surrounding the apartment complex was more than three metres high and while there were bins stacked against it to give him a leg over he did not know what was on the other side. He looked up at the apartment building he had just left. All the windows were shuttered, but that did not mean that someone would not see him, or even already had, and give a description or that someone would see him in the street beyond.

Once again Wolf decided he would have to let fate take a hand and jumped up onto one of the bins. A row of tiles jutted out on either side of the wall and he could feel them wobbling like loose teeth as he pulled himself over them and to his delight a narrow street with cars parked tightly against the other side of the wall. He eased himself over and on to the roof of one of the vehicles and then to the ground before walking – as nonchalantly as can be expected given what he had just seen and done in the last five minutes – down the alley and back onto a main street.

He walked back towards the city centre despite the scorching heat, not daring to look at the printed pages until he had put at least a kilometre between himself and the apartment block. He stepped into a small cafe and ordered a beer before sitting at a table and pulling the sheaf of pages from his pocket. Most of the sheets contained lists of tables, measurements and what appeared to be seismographs, but the last three sheets had a typed summary and although Wolf tried to read over it and assimilate it he could take in nothing.

The fact of Marco's brutal death was bad enough but he was sure that whoever had killed him was also trying to set Wolf up. There was also Kei to consider – Wolf was going to have to break the news to her. He was tempted to order another beer but held back, conscious that he needed to keep a clear head. There was no question of his going back to Ramon's apartment and collecting his overnight bag. Wolf knew that Ramon would quickly realise that he had gone to ground, hopefully thinking it was to avoid the Slovenian authorities rather than because of the brutal murder close to the city centre that was bound to make the news headlines by that evening.

27

LORCAN WAS READING TO IRINDA FROM a book of fairytales a story about one of the best known characters in Irish folklore. Finn McCool was a warrior of the Fianna who are said to have ruled Ireland 2,000 years ago. A whole body of myth and legend, known as the Ossianic Cycle, had grown up around the Fianna, Finn McCool and his son Oisin. As well as being a warrior Finn was a poet and regarded as one of the wisest men in Ireland. However, the story of how Finn came by his knowledge drew on a much more ancient tradition concerning the Salmon of Knowledge. The salmon was a powerful symbol of learning and wisdom in Celtic mythology.

'Finn was sent to learn poetry and science from an old Druid called Finegas who lived beside a river,' read Lorcan. 'A salmon was said to live in this river beneath a hazel tree which grew on the river bank. Nuts from the hazel tree are also associated in Celtic myth with wisdom and the salmon was said to have fed on nuts from this tree when they dropped into the river. Finegas believed that if he could eat this salmon then all its knowledge would be passed onto him and he spent many years trying to catch it. Finally he caught the salmon and he ordered his pupil, Finn, to cook it but warned him not to taste the fish. However, as Finn turned the fish on a spit he burned his thumb and without thinking put it into his mouth. As the boy tasted the flesh of the Salmon of Knowledge all the wisdom passed into him. The moral of the story was that wisdom rarely comes to those who expect to have it but can sometimes come by accident to those who were not even seeking it.

' Irinda took the book from Lorcan and gazed at the pictures in it.

'Very true,' murmured Lorcan to himself, shuddering as he recalled how his mind had been wrenched out of reality and thrust into a new dimension by the LSD he had taken in Berlin 40 years earlier.

He heard a car pulling up outside his house and presumed it was Kei returning. She had left early in the morning, leaving a note to say that she had some business to attend to but would be back that night. As the door opened Kei came in followed by a tall lanky figure dressed in jeans and a green combat jacket. Lorcan looked at the unshaven face and knew that it was his son even before Irinda had flung herself at him. In the fuss that followed Lorcan stayed in the background as the little girl bombarded Wolf with questions about why he had grown his hair and why he had been on television. As Wolf patiently answered them, Lorcan could see that Kei was forcing herself to smile at Irinda's delight at seeing her father again but he thought that she had been crying. He wondered what Wolf had said to her. He felt protective towards Kei and Irinda and felt that Wolf had no right to suddenly descend on them causing disruption and upset. But still he sat silent and watched, occasionally meeting Wolf's eye as they glanced warily at one another.

'Is it OK for Wolf to stay here?' Irinda asked Lorcan.

'Of course he can stay as long as he wants?' replied Lorcan.

'Thank you,' said Wolf, the first direct word he had spoken to his father.

Satisfied with the arrangements Irinda allowed herself to be put to bed by Kei leaving Lorcan and Wolf to sit in silence. Eventually Kei returned and she could sense that there had been no communication since she'd left.

'Did you tell Irinda about Marco?' asked Wolf.

Kei shook her head.

'She's so happy tonight that I didn't want to spoil it for her. We can tell her tomorrow or in a couple of days.'

Lorcan looked to Kei waiting for her to explain what they were talking about but she sat staring into the distance. Wolf came to with a start realising that it would have to be him would enlighten Lorcan. He told him how he had found Marco's mutilated corpse in his Madrid apartment and his belief that someone was trying to frame him for the murder. All the time Wolf was conscious that this was the man who had abandoned his mother before he had even been born. He felt angry at Kei for contacting Lorcan and bringing Irinda to meet him but felt unable to say anything because of the news he had to break to her about Marco.

'Do you think the police in Spain suspect you?' asked Lorcan.

Wolf shrugged.

'I checked with my partner Imma who lives there. She has been keeping an eye on the news for me but she says the police have not released too much information, merely saying that a body has been found and that they believe Marco was the victim of a contract killing. They haven't named any suspects.'

'Imma?' said Kei. 'Is this the same Imma who kept popping in to your life when we were together.'

Wolf nodded and bit his lip, cursing his stupidity for inadvertently revealing his rekindled relationship with Imma before he had time to properly tell Kei. Lorcan sighed as he felt the tension between the various parties but did not want to say anything as his years as a recluse had left him socially awkward at the best of times.

'That's good,' said Kei at last. 'I hope it works out this time.'

Wolf and Lorcan instinctively glanced at one another and read the look of mutual relief in one another's faces, with Lorcan raising his eyebrows and Wolf nodding slowly.

'So then Lorcan how does it feel to have a social pariah for a son?' asked Wolf doing his bit to ease the atmosphere.

'Well … I don't know. I suppose I don't really deserve to call myself your father but I have been trying to do a better job at being a grandfather to Irinda.'

Wolf nodded.

'She seems very fond of you,' he said.

They all sat in silence again nodding at one another. Lorcan was wary about breaking the silence but could not get his head around the fact that someone had tried to frame Wolf for Marco's murder.

'Why would anyone do that?' Lorcan asked at last after he had explained what was perplexing him.

'He had been involved in some very sensitive research on behalf of the company he worked for and had gone to ground,' said Wolf. 'I think that given his past associations with me, via Kei, the company suspected that he was going to hand that information over to me. They wanted to stop him doing so and to discredit me in the most extreme way possible while doing so.'

'What was the information?' asked Kei.

Wolf pulled a bundle of sheets from his rucksack. They were not the original ones he had printed off in Marco's apartment as they might have been traced back to the murder scene. He had gone to a photocopying shop in Madrid and made three copies, sending one to Niels in Amsterdam, one to Madja in Slovenian for safekeeping and held on to a copy for himself. He had then burned the original documents before catching a bus to Santander and then a ferry to England from where he travelled to Ireland.

Kei looked at the documents.

'They look like laboratory results of soil samples,' she said.

'Niels is getting someone to do a more detailed analysis but Marco had already written up a brief summary,' said Wolf.

'And what did it say?'

'I thought he was taking the piss but then I thought who would risk getting themselves killed just to play and elaborate joke on someone. The soil samples were taken from deep beneath the ice that covers the Antarctic. Marco had been part of a scientific expedition working there for six months, although of course as usual that was simply a front for him to carry out research on behalf of AKNR.'

'In the Antarctic!' exclaimed Kei. 'Surely even AKNR don't believe that they would ever be given permission to drill there.'

'I'm confused,' said Lorcan. 'How would a mining company be able to get through all the ice and snow anyway?'

'It would be expensive,' said Wolf. 'But AKNR always somehow manage to latch on to well-funded scientific expeditions which have state-of-the art equipment. It allows them to access detailed geological data from remote parts of the world without incurring any costs and at the same time giving them a cover to explore potential mineral and oil deposits in environmentally sensitive areas.'

'And what did they find?' asked Kei.

'Oil. Huge untapped reserves, according to Marco's report,' said

Wolf. 'It might not be economically viable now but as global reserves are depleted and technology advances they would be eventually able to make a case for drilling it out?'

'But surely there would be an international outcry?' said Lorcan.

'Oh absolutely but in a global economy dependent on fossil fuels the economic argument would soon win through. AKNR are a US company, but the Chinese, Russians, British, Japanese, French and dozens of other countries all have scientific expeditions in Antarctic. Most are genuine but you can be sure that some are scouring for mineral, oil and gas deposits.'

'And you think Marco's bosses had him killed because he was going to give this information to you?' asked Kei.

Wolf nodded.

'But there was more to it than that, although Marco knew that it would be damaging to his company,' he continued. 'It was the by-product of that research that he thought was more interesting and that he thought you should have.'

'Why me?' demanded Kei. 'I'm an archaeologist not a geologist or a miner, why would I be interested in it and if so why did he now give it to me directly?'

'Well its clear that he was taking a considerable risk giving it to anyone in the first place and Marco knew that his employers would take you out as quickly as they did him if they thought you had this material because of your links to me. I suppose Marco felt quite justified putting my life at risk in return for information that would be valuable to environmental campaigners and at the same time knew that I would pass on the additional material to you.'

'What was the additional information?' asked Lorcan.

Wolf smiled enigmatically.

'The upper soil samples, closest to the ice that covered it, contained evidence of plant life but one of the samples contained what appeared to be bone,' he said. 'They initially thought it was the remains of an animal or a bird but when the DNA was analysed it was found to be human.'

'Humans living in the Antarctic. But I thought it had been covered with ice for millions of years,' said Lorcan.

'I'm just telling you what Marco wrote in his summary. As I said Niels is trying to get a more detailed analysis of the data which I sent him.'

'When you say human do you mean protohuman?' asked Kei.

Wolf shook his head.

'No, you can read it for yourself Marco is quite clear. The DNA was from a homo sapien who lived around 14,000 years ago and had similar traits to people found in modern day India.'

'India?' exclaimed Lorcan. 'Are you sure thus wasn't a hoax. The Antarctic ice caps are at least two miles thick and would have taken hundreds of thousands of years, probably millions, to develop. Human beings as a species did not even exist a million years ago.'

Kei shook her head and explained the theories of Charles Hapgood and his conclusion that the Earth's crust had in the past been subjected to sudden and violent displacement. Kei glanced over to Lorcan and was startled by the look that was spreading across his face.

'Are you OK?' she asked, alarmed.

'All those things we have been discussing over the last week, about the dig in the Sahara and the speculation about a lost civilization,' said Lorcan. 'It was just swimming around in my head but it just all seemed to come together.'

Lorcan stared straight ahead for another few minutes.

'Am I missing out on something here?' asked Wolf, confused.

Kei gave him a quick run down on the dig she had been involved in and how she thought it might fit in with her theories about an antediluvian civilization.

Lorcan, gestured to the books and printouts he had been perusing.

'What we have here are the echoes of a global catastrophe whose after effects rippled through the legends and myths of cultures throughout the world. There are thousands of them, on every continent and while there are huge variations the similarity among many of them is striking. Like the Christian Bible the flood is often blamed on a vengeful god who is angry at behaviour of the people he has created and decides to punish them, often only sparing an individual and a small entourage surrounding him. It was a disaster on a horrendous scale affecting every corner of the world. An entire civilization … not just in a single country but spread all over the world was wiped out in an instant in what was probably the modern day equivalent of a nuclear disaster.'

'A global civilization?' asked Wolf

'Not a single culture … a world of nations, like we have today – with different ethnic groups, languages and religions – spread over the world but linked to one another and able to communicate ideas and trade with one another … possibly even going to war at times … technologically advanced, although not as we might understand it with electricity and computers … but in terms of a sophisticated architecture that reflected religious beliefs and cultural motifs. I suspect they would have had music and literature, although it may have been an oral tradition but with a visual aspect. The building you excavated Kei was not just a temple, but an art gallery and concert venue … even a sort of cinema. Those delicate carvings which have survived for so long were designed to shapeshift as the light entering the structure changed, even to suggest subtle changes as people moved around or blinked. People would have sat there for hours letting the various shapes come and go, maybe reciting stories, songs or even prayers as a sort of theme music to what they were seeing. And then it was all wiped out, possibly in a matter of hours. Towns and cities completely destroyed, widespread death and injury leaving just a few survivors. The whole infrastructure in which they had lived to that point was gone. 'Can you imagine if that happened today how people in our so-called civilized society would cope with no shops or supermarkets to buy food, no electricity or gas, maybe no fresh running water and no television, radio or newspapers to even tell them what was going, what to do, where was safe to go? Everything those people had ever known was gone and it was not just a way of life, they would have had to cope with the loss of loved ones on a huge scale, entire families and communities suddenly wiped out. Hundreds of thousands of bodies would have been left unburied, or not cremated or mummified – whatever their funeral rites were – and those who survived would have had to abandon the remains of their towns and cities because of disease and plague. They would have been forced to flee to high grounds to escape the floods and only those who were able to adapt to the new world would have been able to survive.'

'Were you really able to see all this?' asked Kei.

Lorcan tapped his head.

'Not in the literal sense, but I sat and let all the conversations we had and the information that I got from the books you gave me, along with the pictures and film from the dig, mingle and that is the image that emerged. I can't say if that is exactly what happened but I just feel a sense that is what it was like. The fact that myths have been transmitted down through history over many thousands of years and seem to be embedded in the collective memory of humanity give us an inkling of the horror. Those who survived must have been very lonely people moving over the desolated planet. Nearly all traces of civilization would have been wiped out and human evolution would have been set back thousands of years with the descendents of the survivors possibly reverting to hunter gatherers or at most very basic farmers. Maybe, a few enlightened communities remained, probably in the mountains and out of reach of the floods. Here the memory of the civilizations that had been wiped out would have been strongest and maybe some of its technologies would have survived. It was these people and their descendents who when they began to travel out in the world again that became the god-like figures of the Tuatha de Dannan, the Olmnec and Quetzalcoatl. They might have even helped to kick start civilization by sharing their knowledge about farming, irrigation and building techniques. In fact they may even have tried to recreate aspects of their lost civilization by encouraging those who they had come to live among to build copies of the structures that had once dominated their cities and towns. But they were approximations – fantastic edifices that may have astounded the primitive peoples of the world who had forgotten their ancestors' achievements but which were a mere theme-park parody of the originals on which they were based. Who knows, maybe the descendants of those people who built the temple you found in the Sahara Desert came to Ireland and with the help of tribes already living here built Newgrange as a sort of memento – like a Frenchman might create a scale model of the Eiffel Tower to commemorate the great society that his ancestors had once lived in but which had been destroyed by a natural catastrophe.'

'But what could cause the Earth's crust to slip and cause such devastation?' asked Wolf.

'According to the Hapgood theory it could have been a change in the pressure on the Earth's surface,' said Kei. 'The last ice age would have begun around 30,000 years ago and reached its peak about 19,000 years ago when huge ice sheets covered much of north America and this part of northern Europe. Where we are now would have been under two miles of ice at that time. In fact Ireland is still rising out of the sea after been burdened by so much weight for so long. Then the ice caps began to melt very rapidly about 14,000 years ago as the earth's atmosphere suddenly warmed up, releasing huge volumes of water.'

'Would than not explain the flood myths that you were talking about?' asked Wolf.

'No, while that meltdown was rapid in terms of global history we are still talking about centuries and so while it might have been perceptible to humans over a lifetime it would still have been a fairly gradual thing rather than an instantaneous deluge.'

'And do you think that is what triggered the shift in the Earth's crust in the Hapgood theory?' asked Wolf.

'Yes it's possible. There would have been billions of tonnes of ice in the northern hemisphere exerting a huge downward pressure on the Earth's crust and at some point during the melting process it would have been like someone suddenly taking their finger off a gyroscope and causing it to suddenly change direction. The easing of pressure would have reached an optimum point allowing the crust to suddenly slide off at a tangent and settle in its new position hurling entire continents and all that lived on them into chaos.'

'Could it happen again?' asked Lorcan.

'I don't want to be alarmist but it is already,' said Wolf. 'Global warming is a fact and the ice caps are melting both at the North Pole and at the Antarctic South Pole.'

'But surely it is a natural phenomena,' said Lorcan. 'I mean there were no carbon emissions 14,000 years ago to trigger the end of the last ice age. Unless the civilization we are speculating about was far more developed than even Kei and I have been imagining.'

'Yes it is a natural phenomena,' said Wolf. 'But we as humans are contributing to an accelerating it by burning fossil fuels. It has been estimated that temperatures could rise in the next 60 or 70 years by as much as 4 to 6 degrees which will make the planet extremely uncomfortable for many billions of people no matter what else happens. It will also have a severe impact on the ice caps causing them to melt and sea levels to rise and if this Hapgood theory Kei is talking about is correct that could even trigger another sudden slip of the earth's crust over the core of the planet.'

'Another global disaster?' said Lorcan.

Irinda stood at her bedroom door and watched her mother, father and grandfather talking. Despite her age she had been aware that earlier during supper they had been uncomfortable together and she had got up to make sure that they were not fighting. She could sense that the conversation was a serious one but was glad that they all seemed to be getting on and happily went back to bed to think of activities that they could all do together in the coming weeks and months as a family.

PART FOUR

28

TUMA SPURRED HIS CAMEL FORWARD AND passed the
scout who had come to fetch him, calling over his shoulder to
urge his men into battle. The sand was beginning to thin out and
he could see fragile pieces of vegetation clinging to rocks and
even what looked like dry earth. The scout had come back to
their camp two nights earlier with news that he had found what
looked like a settlement with water. He had said that it seemed
to be occupied by just a small tribe but Tuma was not prepared
to take risks, the stakes were too high, and ordered his best
warriors to saddle up. As he looked behind him he was pleased at
what saw – their black robes flowed stark against the desert
landscape and their spears tips glistened in the harsh sunlight.
Tuma hoped that the tribe they were about to attack would
quickly succumb to fear and surrender for while he did not doubt
his men's ability to fight he knew that the shortage of food and
water in the last few weeks had left them below strength. This
settlement was their last hope and unless they conquered it his
own tribe would be forced to pack up their women and children

and move again. It would be the fifth year in a row and each move had had a devastating effect on his people with many falling ill and dying, including Tuma's own father who had led their tribe before him as well as two of Tuma's wives and three of his children. The thought of what he and his people had lost strengthened Tuma's resolve and he roared a battle cry and raised his spear into the air. There were still a few sand dunes and as he rounded one of them he saw an amazing sight – a huge stone structure, shaped in a circle stood before him. He pulled his camel up and could hear his men doing the same behind him and gasping in fear and astonishment. Tuma muttered a quick prayer. He had heard of such places before but only in the myths and legends of his people and had thought they were simply fairytales.

He motioned for his men to spread out, hissing at them to be on constant guard, and then with his two most senior men beside him eased his camel forward. As they got closer they could see a handful of dilapidated huts, their roofs sagging and walls beginning to cave in. In front of one of them sat an old man who gazed at Tuma and his warriors, apparently without fear.

Tuma raised his spear again and roared a threat at the old man but he remained perfectly still.

'Where are your people?' Tuma demanded. 'You must tell them to surrender or be killed.'

The old man frowned slightly as he gazed at Tuma and then shrugged.

'They're all gone and you're too late,' he said

'How am I too late if there is no-one here then we are claiming these lands and everything in them, including that,' said Tuma pointing at the stone structure.'

The old man shrugged again.

'Take it but it won't do you any good. The sand is getting a bit closer every day. This time last year we could see it on the horizon, this year it is at our feet and by this time next year all this will be buried under it.'

Tuma felt his heart sink but he still half hoped that the old man was trying to deceive him. He dug his heels into the camel's sides to make it lower him to the ground and climbed off and pointed his spear at the old man's neck

'Where is your well?' he demanded.

The old man eased himself to his feet and hobbled to an indent in the ground and pointed.

'It used to be there,' he said. 'I can still dig down and get enough water to keep me and a few goats alive but that's it. I doubt there'll be enough to sate the thirst of us both, never mind the rest of your men, or I presume your tribe who you hope to bring here.' Tuma was alarmed.

'How do you know out plans?' he demanded.

'You're not the first to come here,' said the old man. 'Others have come before and they have all moved on, including my own people, and no-one ever comes back so I can only presume they have found somewhere better to be with water and food or else they have died from thirst.'

Tuma felt the hope he'd had drain from him and knew in his heart that the old man was telling the truth. He thrust his hand into the dark earth and felt it moist but knew that even that would soon be evaporated to nothing by the sun and then covered by the sands.

'When did your people leave?' he asked.

'Last year, when we first realised that the sand was moving in our direction. We knew others would come and decided it was best to move ahead. We were a small tribe and knew that others were more powerful than us and I thought that if they went quickly we might find somewhere well ahead of anyone else who followed and have time to establish ourselves and build our strength while those who stayed behind would be weaker and less able to attack us.'

Tuma looked at the old man with new admiration. It was the advice his own father had given him before he had died two years earlier. But Tuma had been so relieved to find an oasis that he had ordered his people to stay only to discover within a few months that the oasis was drying up like all the others they had made camps at over the years and that they would be forced to move again. He feared now that his tribe would be too weak to make the extended move that his father had told him to do and that this old man had told his own people to do. His scouts had been seeking new oases for months now but despite ranging further and further this was all they had come up with and it would take at least a week for the full tribe with its women, children, elderly and infirm to get there.

'Why did you not go with your tribe?' Tuma asked. 'Did they abandon you?'

'No it was my choice,' said the old man shaking his head. 'I wouldn't have lasted too long and at least here I can die and lie beside my ancestors.'

'Did they live in there?' asked Tuma pointing towards the stone structure.

'No. In my time it was place of worship but I think before that in the far past it was a place of record.'

'How do you mean?'

'I can't describe it we no longer have the words to do so but I can show you?'

'How?' demanded Tuma nervously, his suspicions aroused again.

'Bring your guards with you if you want but there is nothing in there that can harm you.'

Tuma was not prepared to show fear but it was with reluctance that he followed the old man towards the stone structure and then with dismay that he saw a darkened opening. Tuma held back, kicking at the layer of sand that had begun to carpet the ground outside the structure, as the old man ducked his head to enter. Tuma looked back at his men and saw that they were more apprehensive than he was. He suspected that some of them had begun to doubt his judgment and so decided it was best not insist that they follow him in, half-hoping that his own bravery in entering might inspire fresh admiration. Perhaps there was even a store of food in there which he could seize and emerge with triumphantly.

The entrance faced away from the sun and inside it was a relief to be out of the constant searing heat. He let his hand run along the cool stone and could feel fine indentations on the otherwise smooth surfaces. Further along the passage there were torches set into the wall giving a little flickering light. In the shadows ahead Tuma could see the old man and he hurried after him with the still vague fear that he might try to ambush him. When Tuma caught up with his guide it was in a place where the passage had opened out into a cavern. He started with fright as he saw what appeared to be five bodies wrapped in cloth lying on a stone altar.

'Who are they?' he demanded.

'My ancestors,' replied the old man.

'Do you not leave your dead out for the vultures to carry away to the next life?' demanded a shocked Tuma.

'We do now but we used to preserve them like this. The science for doing so has been lost to us although I think it may be recorded in here.'

'How can it be recorded?'

The old man beckoned him towards one of the walls and using one of the torches to illuminate it pointed to a series of scratches on the stone. Tuma was baffled.

'What is it?' he asked.

'According to my people's traditions it was in this way that we used to store our knowledge and that if you could understand these signs you could put them into words.'

'I still don't know what you are talking about.'

'I don't know what they mean either. The knowledge has been lost to us. Apart from a few symbols.'

'Symbols?' repeated Tuma, not knowing what the word meant. 'Explain.'

'Here,' motioned the old man, pointing at a series of scratches. 'My grandfather showed me this when I was a boy and told me how to interpret them. According to him these symbolised the sounds that made the name of one of our tribe's elders, my grandfather's father's grandmother?'

'A woman?' snorted Tuma. 'How can they make the sound of a woman's name.'

'This what my grandfather taught me,' insisted the old man.

'And you know these sounds?'

'Not all of them, just these, although I have seen them repeated in other parts of the temple but never in the same order and always mixed up with other scratches.'

'So what are the sounds made by this,' Tuma said pointing.

'That is 'dee'.' but they come in a sequence. Look this is 'eye', that one is 'err', then there is the first one again, 'eye' then this one is 'enn' then that 'dee' and then 'aaah'.

Tuma looked at the old man and wondered if loneliness and the sun had riddled his mind.

'What sort of name is that?' he asked.

'When you say them all one after the other you get the name of my ancestor,' replied the old man.

Tuma tried to follow what he was saying but was baffled.

'What name?' he demanded.

'Irinda,' said the old man.